MURDER SPOILS THE SWEETS

Rooftop Garden Cozy Mysteries, Book 10

THEA CAMBERT

Summer Prescott Books Publishing

CHAPTER 1

"This is disgusting!" Owen James put down his plate and took a huge gulp of coffee. "Ow! Hot!" he cried, putting the coffee down. "Hand me a napkin, Alice, I need to wipe off my tongue."

"What is this made of again?" asked Alice Maguire, grimacing a bit after taking a bite from her plate. "Plums and what else?"

"Technically, there are no plums in plum pudding," said Owen. "This has bread crumbs, spices, dried fruit, and suet."

"Hold on," said Franny Brown-Maguire, sniffing at her plate. "What's suet again?"

"Suet?" asked Alice, setting her plate slowly onto the café table in the rooftop garden the three friends shared. "This has actual suet in it?"

"I repeat, what is suet?" asked Franny.

"Oh, it might have something to do with the solid fat found around certain parts of certain animals," said Owen. He looked at the aghast faces of his friends. "Well, I wanted it to be authentic, okay? Darn. I didn't even set it on fire yet," he said, hands on his hips. He gave a little sniff. "But admittedly, I'm going to need to tweak the recipe a little."

"I just ate lard," said Franny, grimacing.

"If that's an issue for you, you're probably going to want to steer clear of these little mincemeat pies, too," said Owen, picking a tiny, handheld pie out of the bakery box he'd brought upstairs from his bakery, which was located down on the first floor.

The rooftop garden was a haven above Blue Valley's Main Street. Down on the first floor were Alice's bookshop, The Paper Owl; Franny's coffee shop, Joe's; and Owen's bakery, Sourdough. Alice had been the first to move into the tiny apartment above her shop some nine years ago, and from the moment she opened the French doors that led out onto the roof from her tiny, bookshelf-lined living room, she'd seen great potential for a garden.

Before long, Franny had opened Joe's and moved in next door, and not long after that, Owen opened Sourdough and took up residence in the third apartment. All three of the friends loved the rooftop space, and after years of loving cultivation, it was covered with climbing vines on trellises, pots of herbs and flowers, small trees, and Alice's trademark twinkle lights. There was a café table where the friends met for coffee most mornings, or glasses of wine after work. The aromas of fresh books, roasted coffee beans, and warm loaves of bread and cakes wafted up the beautiful old wooden staircase that climbed up from the shared hallway that ran along the back of the building—and the smells were the finishing touch that made the place feel like home.

Just over a year ago, Franny had married Alice's brother Ben, who was Blue Valley's police chief. Then Alice had gotten engaged to Ben's good friend and colleague, Detective Luke Evans. Alice and Luke were set to get married in just over a week, and with Christmas in the air and the annual Christmas festival about to kick off, Alice could feel an almost constant sense of joy bubbling up in her heart. That is, when she wasn't exhausted between last-minute wedding planning, being chair of the festival committee for the third year in a row, and helping Franny and Ben look after their son, Theo.

"Well, we really ought to cut back on the sweets anyway," said Alice. "Since Thanksgiving, I feel like we've been on one long sugar binge."

"That's because we have, between the holiday sweets and testing cakes for your wedding," said Franny.

"We need to recommit to our morning run-walks," said Owen. "Did you see Bella Hendricks out there this morning?"

"Yep," said Alice. "She smoked us."

"Left us in her dust," agreed Franny.

"I wonder if she's entered in tomorrow morning's 5k," said Owen.

"She came in for coffee on Monday," said Franny, nodding. "She told me she's in."

Every year, the town Christmas festival kicked off with a five kilometer fun run. This year, since the theme was Dickens' England, it was the Figgy Pudding 5k Fun Run. Participants would have to overcome several obstacles on their way to the finish line, including the ultimate test of slogging through a vat of sticky figgy pudding for the win.

"Well then, I bet Bella will smoke us again in the morning," said Alice with a laugh.

"Good thing we're not going for speed," said Owen, taking a bite of the mince pie he still held. He looked at Alice. "I'm glad the festival committee decided to go with a Charles Dickens-themed event this year, but getting the desserts of Victorian England adjusted for a Tennessee Smoky Mountain palate isn't easy."

"But you're a brilliant baker," said Alice, patting Owen on the shoulder. "I know you'll get it just right."

"And I'll also get your wedding cake just right," said Owen, smiling.

"I don't doubt that for a moment," said Alice. "Every sample you've made has been amazing."

Owen was an artist with baked goods of all kinds, but cakes were definitely one of his specialties. He'd presented more cupcake-sized samples of wedding cake and frosting combinations than Alice cared to count, but she'd enjoyed every single one. They'd settled on her favorite: a butter almond cake with a rich white chocolate filling. Owen refused to reveal his plan for the design, but Alice knew it would be a reflection of his perception of her, and she couldn't wait to see it.

"So, what's on tap for today?" asked Franny, taking a sip of coffee.

"Let's see . . ." said Alice. "Work at the shop this morning, then after lunch, we go to my wedding gown fitting, and right after that, we have our final festival meeting. Did you both take the afternoon off?"

"The whole weekend, basically," said Owen, and Franny nodded too. "I've got Hilda coming in at noon. You know how grumpy she gets whenever there's a festival going on. She's basically in a bad mood until after New Year's."

"But man, can she bake," said Franny.

"She's a loveable little curmudgeon," said Alice.

"Are Lexi and Zack in town?" asked Owen, looking at Alice.

"Yep," said Alice. "They're done with their fall semester and here until mid-January. Lacie is, of course, performing in *A Christmas Carol*, but her call times aren't until the evenings after the shop is closed. They said they want all the work hours they can get, so I have them coming in today at lunchtime and staying on duty all weekend."

Lacie and Zack, a longtime couple, attended college in a nearby town where Lacie was a theater arts major. But thankfully for Alice, they often came home on weekends and never missed a town festival.

"Beth's taking on extra hours, too," said Franny. "She loves festivals, because the shop stays busy all day and she likes meeting new customers, but she wants to be in the coffee shop, rather than out on Main Street. And between your parents and mine, Theo is booked all weekend too. I don't know what I'm going to do with all the free time!"

Alice took out her giant Christmas festival planning binder and scanned her checklist. "Oh, there'll be plenty for you to do. Let's see . . . we've got the fun run in the morning. The Blakes are handling the vat of figgy pudding and Mrs. Howard has a group of volunteers coming from the high school to set up the obstacles and monitor the course. We've booked the Gothic Trolls to carol all weekend . . ."

The Gothic Trolls were Blue Valley's favorite musical group. They were one of the highlights of the annual medieval fair every spring. Alice couldn't wait to see them all decked out in their Dickens costumes, singing traditional Christmas carols.

"The Holly and the Ivy Maze runs all weekend. We've got Norm and Pearl Ann overseeing that. And we'll have horse-drawn sleigh rides around town and out to the clearing all weekend, too," Alice continued.

"It's so cool that you found sleighs with wheels," said Franny.

"Who knows? Maybe we'll even get some snow this weekend," said Owen.

"There's a good chance," said Alice. "A front's supposed to blow in on Thursday night, but it might rain before it snows."

"Maybe we'll even have a white Christmas this year!" said Franny.

"We have the Dickens Christmas Merry Market on Main Street all weekend. And of course, the play, *A Christmas Carol*, will run Thursday, Friday, and Saturday nights," Alice finished, snapping her notebook shut.

"Chester's in rare form this year from what I hear," said Owen, laughing. "He still finds new ways to ham it up after all these years."

Chester Lehman played the role of Scrooge every year and was brilliant at it. He'd been a bit of a Scrooge in real life until he'd fallen in love with his old friend and Alice and Ben's grandmother, Georgina. Now Granny and Chester were happily settled in their cottage on Azalea Street, a block off Main, and Alice had been relieved that even though Chester was over the moon these days, he could still channel his inner Scrooge when needed.

"I wish Michael wasn't out of town," said Alice, turning to Owen.

"Me too," said Owen. "But he's going to try to get home in time for your wedding."

Michael Boyd was a dear friend. He was the concierge at the Blue Valley Great Granddaddy Mountain Preserve and Resort Lodge—a.k.a. the Lodge. He was also a brilliant poet and a sensitive soul, and was so perceptive that he'd even been instrumental in helping the friends solve crimes from time to time. As to crime, there wasn't a lot of it in Blue Valley. But with all of the tourists who constantly flowed into and out of town, there were bound to be issues sometimes, and Alice, Franny, and Owen had proven themselves on more than one occasion to be quite the crime-solving team. Ben and Luke, along with the rest of the town's little police force, did an amazing job . . . but everyone needs a little help now and again, and Alice, Franny, and Owen often couldn't stifle their curiosity enough to leave well enough alone—even though they'd been warned to stay out of the way more than once.

Franny absently took a bite of her plum pudding. "Ugh! I didn't mean to do that!" She took a quick swig of coffee. "You know what we should do? Get a jump start on our New Year's resolution to eat healthier and get fit. Let's not wait until January."

Alice and Owen looked at Franny, then at each other, and after a moment's thought, nodded in agreement.

"How do we get started?" asked Owen.

"We start by tweaking our diets," said Franny.

"Right before Christmas?" said Alice with a groan.

"No time like the present," said Franny. "Besides, we're not cutting out all sweets. We're just curbing them a little, and getting more active."

"And you know, there are some really amazing healthy options out there these days," said Owen. "We should walk down to the Good Earth Emporium today when we break for lunch."

"That's a great idea!" said Alice. "We can drop in there before my dress fitting."

"You're on!" said Franny. "We'll stock up on healthy snacks to keep ourselves in line this weekend."

CHAPTER 2

Main Street was still fairly quiet at noon when the three friends left their helpers in charge of their respective shops and strolled along, stopping now and then to say hello to friends and fellow shopkeepers.

"It's the calm before the storm," said Owen, as they helped Marge Hartfield, owner of the Waxy Wick candle shop, lug heavy boxes of her Christmas candles out to the booth she and Koi Butler, Blue Valley's favorite yoga teacher, were setting up and stocking for the Merry Market.

"Yep," said Marge. "I hear all the inns and campsites are booked solid beginning tonight. By tomorrow morning, this will be a whole different street!"

"These candles smell amazing, Marge!" said Franny, whose heightened sense of smell was legendary in the little town. "Is that *snow* I smell?" Franny pulled a candle out of the box and smelled it again. "It *is* snow! Snow and . . . cream and vanilla?"

"Astounding!" said Marge. "Exactly right, Franny. That's our

Holiday Snowball candle. Koi and I created that one together."

Koi's yoga studio, Breathe, was located in the back section of the Waxy Wick, and he and Marge were neighbors as well, living in the building's upstairs apartments. Marge didn't have any children of her own, and was thrilled that young Koi had taken such an interest in becoming a candle maker, as generations of Hartfields had done before Marge.

"Look at this!" said Alice, picking through another box of candles. "Marge has created a whole line of Dickens-inspired candles."

"Yep," said Marge proudly. "They're all based on *A Christmas Carol*."

"Ooh! *Fezziwig's Favorite* smells like a Christmas party," said Owen, taking deep whiff.

"Not to be confused with *Ghost of Christmas Present*," said Marge, nodding. "*Fezziwig's* has top notes of cloves and burning oak wood. Then there is a rum punch mid note."

"And we threw a little gingerbread into the base notes," said Koi.

Franny had picked up a *Ghost of Christmas Present* candle and taken a whiff. "I smell cinnamon, nutmeg, a little musk," she said. "And something else . . . Is that holly blossom?"

"Well done, Franny!" said Marge.

"These are wonderful, Marge and Koi," Alice said. "I bet you'll sell out, as usual."

She ordered a few sets of the Dickens candles to sell in The

Paper Owl, and then they walked on down Main Street, hung a right on Trillium and a left on Azalea.

"I hope I can get Peyton to give me a hint about how she makes the delicious gluten-free bread she sells at the Emporium," said Owen. "It's so good."

"You're the king of gluten, Owen," said Alice with a laugh. "You don't have a gluten restriction. What are you doing eating gluten-free bread?"

"Because everyone's always talking about how amazing Peyton's is. Naturally, I had to taste it." He shook his head. "I've tried a million different variations in my bakery, and I just can't get a loaf to turn out as moist and flavorful as Peyton's. Mine are always dry and crumbly."

"So, you're hoping she'll tell you her secret?" asked Franny, grinning.

"Maybe I could give her my plum pudding recipe in exchange," said Owen.

"Yeah, right." Alice rolled her eyes at him and pulled open the door of the Good Earth Emporium.

Peyton and Sonny Kingsley, the store owners, greeted them.

"What can we help you with today?" asked Sonny.

"We're stocking up on healthy snacks," said Alice.

"In that case, taste this," said Peyton, lifting a large glass dome off a dish of iced gingerbread snowflake cookies.

Alice took a bite. "Delicious!" she said.

"These taste like my mom's gingerbread," added Franny. "And they're so pretty."

"You're not going to tell us these are health food, are you?" asked Owen.

Peyton laughed. "If only! But they are better for you than the average cookie. They're made with organic, whole-grain wheat, molasses, spices—just a few simple ingredients."

"And they're on sale today," added Sonny, motioning toward a display piled high with the cookies, all neatly wrapped in festive bags for gift-giving.

"Franny, get a cart," said Owen. "We're going to need it."

For the next fifteen minutes, they walked up and down the aisles, filling their cart with things like organic cheddar popcorn, low-salt roasted nuts, locally sourced baby vegetables, and homemade hummus to dip them in. There were cruelty-free organic cheeses and ancient grain crackers. There were even matcha-cocoa cupcakes with thick, organic cream cheese frosting laced with green tea and unfiltered honey.

"Are you all having a party or something?" asked Peyton as she rang up their purchases and packed them into the store's signature compostable paper bags.

"We're just arming ourselves for the holiday," said Alice. "We know we'll be more likely to cut back on junk food if we have healthier alternatives at the ready."

"Good for you," said Peyton.

"If you want to take your health goals a step further," said Sonny, stepping up to the counter, "consider stopping by the new shop next door."

"I noticed someone had moved in there," said Alice. "Who is it?"

"It's called The Daily Dose. Owned by a friend of ours, Elmer Smallweed. He's an expert in the fields of nutrition and supplementation. Sonny's helping him get up and running—and helping out in the shop whenever he can."

"Oh—I know Elmer," said Owen. "He's also a friend of Faith Lindor, who owns Crumpets. She's always giving him complementary scones—never lets him pay."

"Lucky man," said Peyton with a smile.

Crumpets was just down Main Street from Sourdough, and where Owen specialized in cakes, cookies, and bread, Faith mostly sold scones, muffins, bagels, and of course, crumpets. Owen had gotten to be good friends with Faith through the years, and they often helped each other out and swapped recipes.

Alice, Owen, and Franny thanked the Kingsleys and headed next door to The Daily Dose.

A pink-cheeked man with neatly styled gray hair wearing khaki pants and a tweed jacket looked up from a laptop computer as they entered. "Welcome!" he said, stepping out from behind the counter. "Welcome to The Daily Dose. How can I help you today?"

"Hello Mr. Smallweed," said Owen, extending his hand. "We've met before through a mutual friend—Faith Lindor."

"Of course! You own the other bakery in town. Sourdough."

"That's right," said Owen. "I'm Owen James. These are my friends Alice and Franny."

"So nice to meet you all. And please, call me Elmer." He smiled broadly at the trio, then glanced at the Good Earth

Emporium bags they carried. "Are we on the market for good health today?"

"We were just next door buying snacks," said Alice. "Sonny and Peyton told us about your shop and we thought we'd stop by."

"I'm so glad you did," said Elmer.

"Wow," said Owen, who was standing next to the *Guess How Many Vitamins Are in the Jar* display. "There must be a million vitamins in there. Look at all the pretty colors."

"Make your guess and write it down on the list along with your name and email address," said Elmer with a grin. "You could win free supplements for a year!"

They spent the next half hour talking about diet and nutrition and health goals. Alice, Owen, and Franny answered Elmer's questions about their lifestyle, including eating and exercise habits, and then discussed goals.

"You're all, what? In your early thirties?" asked Elmer.

"That's right," said Owen.

"You need to be thinking about tweaking your diets, staying active. And if you want to ensure that everything is balanced, you might consider a few supplements—nothing too crazy. Just an all-natural, plant-derived multi, to cover your nutritional bases. Maybe a good, solid probiotic and a daily dose of omegas for heart health. You'd be surprised how well high-quality supplements can fill the gaps in our diets. And believe me, we all have gaps." With that, he invited them to look around the store and gave them a flyer about his *New Year New You* program that would be taking place in early January. "There'll be plenty of steals and deals in the shop."

Alice liked it that Elmer hadn't pressured them to make a purchase that day, and also that he offered plenty of reading materials about nutrition and exercise. After they'd thanked him and taken the free sample goodie bag he handed over, they headed toward the exit, noticing a particularly striking display next to the door.

"Nutrique," Owen read from the gleaming sign above the display. "Your life. Balanced."

"The packaging is gorgeous," said Alice, picking up a bottle of something called Peak Performance and turning it over in her hands. "This one is for athletes," she said.

"Or people who want to *become* athletes," said Elmer from behind them. "Our Nutrique line is the centerpiece of this shop. These are my own personal formulations." He pointed to various colorful bottles on the display. "We have supplements to help your hair grow thick and shiny, clear up your skin, smooth out your wrinkles, to help you attain your ideal weight, or help you build muscle or have more energy. There are so many ways to improve your health and the quality of your life through good, solid science." He handed them each a shiny Nutrique brochure. "Take these home and look them over," he said. "Then come to my healthy living seminar early in the new year. We can work out a program tailored to your personal goals. The consultation will be absolutely free, and there's never any pressure to buy anything."

"Sounds great," said Franny, looking at her brochure.

"Thanks, Elmer," said Alice.

They left The Daily Dose feeling inspired and motivated.

"We're going to have lush hair, smooth skin, and tons of energy," said Owen. "What more could we want?"

"For my wedding gown to fit," said Alice. "Time for my appointment at Celebrations Boutique."

With that, Owen launched into his own rendition of the wedding march and they headed back up Main Street.

CHAPTER 3

"Alice, it's gorgeous!" said Franny, when Alice came out of the fitting room and stepped up onto the alterations platform, which was surrounded by mirrors so that the bride-to-be could inspect her gown from every angle.

Becky Watters, owner of Celebrations Boutique and seamstress extraordinaire, gave a round of applause. "Just a few more tiny adjustments and it'll be perfect."

"You're the one who deserves the applause, Becky," said Alice. "I can't get over how beautiful it is."

Alice's gown was stunning, from its hand-sewn, fitted silk bodice to its sweeping skirt, scattered with tiny silvery beads that caught in the light for a magical effect. The bodice was topped with a semi-sweetheart strapless neckline, and one of the gown's most striking features was the swath of sheer chiffon that draped over Alice's right shoulder and then tied seamlessly into the back. The full effect was at once classically simple and fairy-tale dreamy, which suited Alice perfectly.

The front door of the shop swung open and Bea Maguire, Alice's mother, hurried in. When she saw Alice, her hands flew to her cheeks and tears sprung to her eyes. "My precious girl!" she said, beaming. "I can't believe my baby is getting married!"

"Mom, you've been after me to find Mr. Right since I was twenty-four. This is a long time coming," said Alice with a laugh.

"I know," said Bea with a sniffle. "But now that it's finally happening, it seems like . . . well . . . I'm looking at you, standing there in that glorious gown, but I still see my little girl."

Alice heard a stifled sob coming from behind her and turned to see Owen, who had found a box of tissues and was wiping his eyes and blowing his nose. He held the box out to Bea, who came and joined him and Franny on the couch.

Becky set about making tiny adjustments to the gown, pinning bits of fabric here and there, inspecting the placement of the beads. "It's lovely that you're getting married outside," she said. "These silvery beads in the sunlight will have a sort of shimmery, icy effect."

"Wait until you see what I'm going to do with Alice's hair," said Franny, who had always loved to play with Alice's long, auburn curls. "And Violet is doing a crown of sprigged pine, blue spruce, and juniper, with those dark blue berries—that'll be Alice's 'something blue'."

Violet Garcia, owner of Violet's Blooms and Bouquets, was an artist with flowers in the same way that Becky Watters was an artist with silk and chiffon. She was creating the wintery crown for Alice, along with a matching boutonniere

for Luke, and she'd chosen tiny burgundy roses for Franny's dark hair and a rose-and-pine mixture for Owen's boutonniere.

"Luke has been working for a month to build an outdoor stone fireplace at the cabin on the lake," said Alice, feeling her heart swell at the thought of her fiancé. "We'll get married right there on the water, and our guests can stand around the fire with hot mulled wine and cocoa after the ceremony." She sighed contentedly.

The shop door opened again and Granny walked in, spotted Alice, and put a hand over her heart. "Oh, Alice," she said, a huge smile on her face. "If ever a gown was more suited to a bride, I haven't seen it. This is perfect!" She came and stood next to her granddaughter. "I'm so glad you've found love."

Alice felt tears stinging her own eyes now. Owen hopped up and handed her a tissue.

"I brought a little something for you," said Granny, handing Alice a parcel wrapped in crinkly brown paper and tied with string. "It can be your 'something old' if you like it."

Alice untied the string and folded back the paper to reveal a creamy cashmere wrap. "Granny! I love it!" she said. "I was wondering how I'd stay warm during our reception. This is perfect."

"I wore it when I married your grandfather, if you can believe it. I'd planned to give it to my son's bride—" at this she smiled at Bea. "But they got married in June, and there wasn't much call for cashmere."

"Put it on, Alice," said Owen, coming to stand next to the platform.

Alice wrapped the cloud of soft fabric around her shoulders and felt instantly enveloped in warmth.

"Classic choice, Granny," said Owen—who himself was as much a part of the Maguire family as anyone else. "You can just wrap it loosely around your shoulders like this, or we could pin it closed with a gorgeous statement brooch."

Becky ran to the jewelry section of the boutique and brought back a sparkling brooch that—although new—looked like a vintage antique. "This would be perfect with your gown," she said.

"This is my 'something new'!" said Alice. "I'll take it!"

"Now all you need is something borrowed," said Owen, clapping gleefully.

Alice carefully stepped down from the platform, and Franny went with her into the large dressing room to help her get out of the gown without messing up the pins or getting poked. When they came back out, Becky was serving delicate pale pink macarons and lightly sweetened chamomile tea in china teacups. They all took seats on the couches and talked about weddings and flowers and cakes, and soon found themselves laughing and smiling over memories of first meetings, first dates, and proposals. Somehow, the discussion found its way back to the Christmas festival and the last-minute preparations they were undertaking before it began the next morning. And that brought them to the first event of the day, which would be the Figgy Pudding 5k Fun Run.

"I'll never quite understand why people find it enjoyable to do these silly obstacle courses," said Bea. "But your dad and I will be waiting at the finish line with our grandbaby." She reached over and patted Franny's knee.

The fun run began and ended at Town Park, and the Maguires still lived in their cozy cottage across the street from the park —the same house that Alice and Ben had grown up in. Franny's parent's, Arthur and Pippa Brown, lived exactly one block away on Azalea Street, right next door to Granny and Chester.

"How's Chester doing as Scrooge this year?" asked Becky, turning to Granny. "I hear this year's show will be the best yet."

"Oh, Chester is in his element on that stage," said Granny with a laugh. "But between that and being so busy at his hardware store, that man is going to need a vacation after the holiday season!"

"I bet Elmer Smallweed has an energizing supplement," said Owen.

"Elmer Smallweed?" asked Granny.

"He owns that new vitamin shop down the street from you," said Alice. "The Daily Dose?"

"Oh, yes," said Granny. "Next to Good Earth Emporium."

"Right," said Alice. "We went there just before coming here. We were really impressed with the place. He's even going to be teaching a seminar about nutrition and vitamins after New Year's."

"I don't know about vitamins and supplements," said Granny, shaking her head. "Doc Howard tells Chester and me to get our vitamins from healthy foods. Well, except we do take fish oil and probiotics. But I don't go in for those so-called natural supplements that are supposed to help you have more energy. A cup of Franny's coffee does that for me, and tastes good to boot." She smiled at Franny.

"Another one of my brides-to-be, Bella Hendricks, swears by Elmer's Nutrique line," said Becky. "She's taking the weight loss formula to drop a few pounds before her wedding in February. She says it's working."

"We saw her out running this morning," said Owen. "She looks fabulous."

"And she's fast," added Franny.

Alice glanced at her watch. "Oh, boy, we're going to be late," she said, setting her tea cup back on the tray and standing. "We have our last-minute preparations meeting for the festival at the Community Center. It starts in three minutes."

"And you *are* the chairperson," said Owen, getting up.

"And you two *are* my able-bodies assistants," said Alice, raising a brow at Owen and Franny. She gave Bea and Granny quick pecks on their cheeks. "Thanks for coming Mom and Granny. Becky, when should I pick up the gown?"

"Saturday morning," said Becky. "I'll have it ready and waiting."

"Thanks, Becky!"

Alice and Franny hurried out the door and Owen, who had stopped to grab the bags from the Green Earth Emporium, had to jog to catch up. "Too bad I can't run like Bella Hendricks!" he said, out of breath.

"Nonsense," said Alice. "Slow and steady wins every time."

CHAPTER 4

"Alice, you've got this festival-planning thing down to an artform," said Owen when they'd returned to their rooftop garden that evening. "Mayor Abercrombie is going to have you running the whole town before long!"

"Just imagine what kind of binder I'd have to lug around if he did that!" said Alice, dropping the giant planning binder onto the café table with a thud.

Alice poured them each a glass of wine, and she and Franny settled in around the fire ring while Owen got the fire going. Alice's cat, Poppy, wound around Owen's legs until he scooped her up and gave her a good scratching behind the ears. Then he set her in Alice's lap and walked to the building's façade that looked down over Main Street.

"You can tell our tourists have arrived," he said, looking down. "Main Street is getting busy. Is that—it is! Bella Hendricks is out jogging *again*. What has gotten into that woman?"

Alice handed Poppy off to Franny and joined Owen. "She must really want to get in shape before her wedding."

"Hope she saves some energy for the fun run tomorrow morning," said Franny.

"Wow. Looks like there's a waiting list at the Smiling Hound." Alice nodded toward the beautiful old building that housed the town's favorite pub, which was just across the street and up a few doors. At that moment, there was a small group of people standing around outside the pub's door, most of them chatting or idly looking at their cell phones. Every now and then, Patrick Sullivan, owner of the Smiling Hound, would stick his head out the door and call another cluster of customers to come inside.

"Patrick's going to be doing a big business all weekend," said Owen, "between the pub and his special booth at the festival —the Christmas Hound."

"Look, there go Ben and Luke," said Alice, pointing to where her brother and fiancé were approaching the Smiling Hound. A moment later, they'd gone inside.

"Good thing we're getting dinner to-go tonight," said Franny, coming to stand with Alice and Owen at the façade. "No waiting for a table."

"*And* we have our own dedicated delivery men," Alice added with a giggle as Ben and Luke emerged from the pub carrying several large bags of food. Luke spotted Alice, Owen, and Franny looking down at them and yelled hello since his hands were too full to wave.

"I'm glad we're all staying on Main for the weekend," said

Owen. "I love being here when a special event is going on in town."

"I never get tired of looking down on this street when the Christmas lights and decorations are up," agreed Alice. "But the lake is amazing, too, with all the colorful lights on everyone's docks reflecting on the water's surface. And it's so peaceful there. I love that—but I also love the holiday bustle here. I'm glad we don't have to choose one or the other."

Alice's brother had grown up dreaming of living out on Blue Lake, so once he'd moved up the ladder enough in the police department, he took the nest egg he'd been sitting on for years and purchased a charming little house on the water. Then, when Luke had moved to town and hung out a few times at Ben's cabin, he quickly fell in love with the crystal clear water framed by the ancient Smoky Mountains, so had gladly purchased and fixed up the little cabin that lay just a stone's throw away from Ben's place, via a winding path through the trees. Then, some months ago, fate had blessed them all when an old cottage just around the bend from Luke's cabin had gone on the market. Owen had snapped it up and spent months lovingly renovating and restoring it, and had moved in just in time for Thanksgiving.

As soon as Alice married Luke, the three friends would officially be neighbors, both on Main Street above their shops, and at Blue Lake in their respective homes. Everyone was tickled pink with this arrangement—and they tended to spend their weeknights out at the lake, and then come into town on weekends or whenever there was a fun downtown event happening in Blue Valley. Of course, the lake was only about a mile from the center of town, so a short bike ride could take them from one location to the other with ease, and nobody had a commute to work of more than a few minutes—or even a few seconds—depending on where they were staying.

Ben and Luke emerged from Alice's apartment and the friends all sat down to a delicious dinner of thick, juicy burgers, fish and chips, steaming beef stew, and the Smiling Hound's famous crispy onion rings.

"I thought we were trying to eat healthier," said Franny, looking at the onion ring in her hand.

"We are," said Alice. "That's why we got the *small* order of onion rings instead of the large."

"And besides, we're carb-loading for tomorrow morning's race," said Owen.

"How was your final festival planning meeting?" asked Luke, spooning up a big bite of beef stew.

"Great," said Alice. "I finally learned—on this, my third year as chair of the festival—that the key to success is delegation."

"That's right," said Owen. "She's been delegating tasks left and right. It's like she has this army of Christmas elf-minions."

"The police department will be patrolling the event all weekend," said Ben. "With so many tourists in town, things can get a little crazy."

"Are you on duty tomorrow night?" asked Franny.

"Yep," said Ben, nodding at Luke.

"Darn," said Franny. "I was hoping you'd be able to go with us to the maze."

"Ah, yes," said Luke. "The Holly and the Ivy Maze. Tell us more about that."

"It's the thing I'm the most excited about all weekend," said Alice. "It's over in the clearing by the lake. There's a vendor who comes in and sets the whole thing up. They brought in these amazing walls covered with holly and ivy, and they've set up this intricate maze."

"And Alice had the idea of putting Charles Dickens' three ghosts inside the maze," said Owen. "When you find a ghost, he or she gives you a sprig of holly."

"And if you manage to collect all three, you're entered into a drawing for all sorts of great prizes," said Franny.

"I'll go ahead and admit the whole thing has me a little spooked," said Owen. "I mean, it's going to be dark—"

"There will be faux torches and candles scattered throughout the maze," said Alice.

"And those ghosts—especially that creepy one," Owen went on.

"The Ghost of Christmas Future?" asked Franny.

"The one with the hood and the scythe," said Owen. "He's like a scary grim reaper. He never talks, either. Just points his boney finger at things. I have no desire to have a run-in with that guy in the dark in a maze that I can't find my way out of. It's like a bad dream."

"Don't worry. We'll stay together the whole way through," said Franny.

Alice nodded and patted Owen on the back. "And it's not like we're going to see any real ghosts," she said with a laugh.

CHAPTER 5

Thursday morning dawned cold and clear—the perfect weather for the first day of the Dickens Christmas Festival. Alice, Owen, and Franny bundled up and headed off to the park where the fun run would begin.

"So, what are the obstacles on the race course this year?" asked Owen as they walked down Main Street.

"No idea," said Alice. "I delegated the whole thing."

"That puts us at a distinct disadvantage," said Owen. "This could get ugly."

"Well, it's definitely going to get sticky," said Franny, eyeing the giant vat of figgy pudding that stood next to the finish line.

"All I know is we start right here at the park, circle around downtown, and end up right back here. The figgy pudding is the final obstacle," said Alice.

"I have a bad feeling about this," said Owen, walking closer to the giant vat, which had wide ramps on either side, so that runners could run up, jump in, and go out the other side to finish the race.

"Look—there's Bella," said Alice, waving at Bella Hendricks, who was just jogging up.

"Hey guys," Bella greeted them. "Ready to run?"

"Not as ready as you are," said Owen, yawning.

"You've really been getting in shape, Bella," said Alice. "You look great."

"It's all thanks to Nutrique," said Bella. "Have you been into The Daily Dose yet?"

"We stopped in yesterday," said Alice. "We had a nice chat with Elmer Smallweed."

"That man knows everything about nutrition," said Bella. "He took the time to sit down with me and discuss my goals in detail. Then he created a regimen tailored just to me. I feel great and have more energy than ever before!"

"I was at Celebrations for my gown fitting yesterday," said Alice. "Becky said you're getting married soon, too."

"I am," said Bella. "That's how my whole health and fitness journey started. I wanted to get in shape for the wedding. Now I have a whole new lifestyle! Well, better go warm up!" She gave them a wave and bounded off.

"Good luck in the race!" Franny called after her.

"Warm up?" said Owen, yawning again and pulling his fleece jacket a little closer around himself. "Should we be doing that too?"

"Nah," said Alice. "We're going to take our time on the race-course. We can warm up during the first mile."

But unfortunately, Bobbie, the owner of Blue Valley Fit, had turned up and insisted on leading the whole group of race participants in a warm-up that included moves like Snow Angel Jumping Jacks and Santa's Squats and worst of all, the Mrs. Claus Cha-Cha-Cha.

After everyone was good and embarrassed, Mayor Abercrombie and his assistant Jake Shannon bustled up to the microphone in the gazebo, welcomed everyone to the Christmas festival, and then proceeded to fire the start gun.

The pack of racers took off down Trillium and hung a left onto Trout Lily.

Almost three miles later, Alice, Owen, and Franny made the final turn back onto Trillium, and the vat of figgy pudding came into view. By that time, they'd triumphed over numerous challenges along the race route. First, they'd encountered *Jacob Marley's Ghostly Chase*, where they were pursued at top speed by Jacob and his ghostly minions. Then there was *Fezziwig's Party*, where they were showered with colorful powders in every bright hue imaginable. There was *Tiny Tim's Snowball Fight*, where they were pelted with a barrage of snowballs. And finally, they'd had to swing on a rope over *Bob Cratchit's Pit of Christmas Custard*. This was where they learned that only Franny had the ability to cling to a rope in motion, and Alice and Owen both ended up in the pit and dripping with custard.

The figgy pudding was thick and sticky, but after a short struggle, they all emerged victorious, looking somewhat the worse for wear, but laughing at themselves and glad they'd conquered the course. Race participants were given warm washcloths and disposable, insulated blankets to wrap up in while they hit the water and snack tables.

A short while later, the awards were announced, with prizes for the fastest runners in every age division, along with prizes for The Stickiest, The Last But Not Least, and Spirit of Christmas. Owen managed to win for being the stickiest runner in the lot, and proudly accepted his medal. They also cheered as Bella accepted her age division award. After she'd had her photo taken with Mayor Abercrombie, who was doing the presenting, she jogged over and joined Alice, Owen, and Franny at the snack table, and picked up a hot cup of coffee.

"Congratulations, Bella!" said Alice. "You were really fast today."

"I set a personal record," said Bella, sipping her coffee. "I feel like I could run the whole thing again right now!" Her smile suddenly faltered a bit. "I feel—" The cup of coffee fell from her hand and splattered on her feet. "I—" Bella's eyes rolled back in her head, and she slumped toward the ground —Owen stepping in just in time to break her fall.

Luckily Doc Howard, who'd run the race that morning as well, was standing nearby and rushed over. He checked Bella's eyes and pulse.

"Her heart is racing," he said. "Call an ambulance."

The hospital was on Phlox Street, a little over a block away, so within a very few minutes, the ambulance had pulled up, and Doc had helped the paramedics get Bella inside and then he climbed into the back with her. They sped away, leaving the rest of the race participants standing by quietly. Alice heard someone calling Bella's fiancé, Lance, on the phone and telling him to get over to the hospital.

"I wonder what happened to Bella," said Owen, pulling his silvery blanket closer around himself as a chill wind swept through the park.

"I'm texting Ben right now," said Franny. "I bet he can find out how she's doing."

They walked back to mid Main Street, and went straight up to their apartments to take long, soapy showers and put on clean, warm clothes. After some breakfast and hot cups of tea, they checked in at their shops and then walked outside to the Dickens Christmas Merry Market. Their whole block of Main Street had been blocked off to traffic for the weekend, and all sorts of vendor booths now lined the sides of the street, while cozy benches, Old World streetlights, and Christmas trees were scattered through the middle. Sleigh rides came and went from the corner of Main and Phlox, taking customers out around Blue Lake and then bringing them back.

At the market, festival goers could purchase anything from imported handmade toys and ornaments to decorated Christmas cookies to bouquets of sparkling balloons. Alice, Owen, and Franny were soon loaded down with shopping bags filled with gifts for everyone on their lists, and they were ready for a break. As they walked toward the Christmas Hound to purchase hot cocoa served up in this year's Blue Valley Christmas Festival commemorative mug, Franny's phone dinged.

"Good news," she said, reading the text message. "Ben says Bella has stabilized."

"Does he say what happened to her?" asked Alice.

"He says they're still waiting on her blood test results," said Franny. "But that she was badly dehydrated and had seriously overdone it."

"Thank goodness she's okay," said Alice.

"This calls for a toast," said Owen, as they approached the Hound. "Patrick my good man, we'll take three hot cocoas in Christmas mugs, and don't skimp on the marshmallows."

"Right away," said Patrick with a little salute. He filled the mugs, added the marshmallows, and handed them over. "May this warm you right through to the cockles of your heart."

"Everything sounds better in that Irish accent of yours, Patrick," said Owen, paying for the cocoa.

"Doesn't it, though?" said Patrick, grinning. He turned and smiled at Peyton and Sonny Kingsley, who were just walking up. "What can I get you two?" he asked.

"We'll have the cocoa," said Peyton, holding up two fingers while Sonny dug in his pocket for his wallet.

"I can't get over your booth this year, Patrick," said Alice. "No wonder you took first prize in the Main Street decorating contest."

"I went all out this year," admitted Patrick. "I studied the Victorian Era extensively at university here in the states, and spent a good deal of time in England as a lad because my father's work took us there. So, when you told me this year's festival was Dickens-themed, I decided to pull out all the stops."

Patrick had decked both his sidewalk booth and the Smiling

Hound pub behind it in bountiful evergreen wreaths and garlands. There were little British flags hanging everywhere, and Patrick wore a black Victorian top hat with a sprig of bright holly in the band. In addition to all of this, the Smiling Hound had sponsored a rather extensive walk-through display highlighting life in Victorian England, and an actor with a long gray beard stood by, showing visitors through the display and intermittently performing dramatic recitations of classic Christmas poems and literary passages.

At the moment, he was bellowing, "Ring out, wild bells, to the wild sky, the flying cloud, the frosty light!"

Owen leaned closer to Patrick and lowered his voice. "What's with that weird Santa guy?"

"What?" Patrick scratched his stubbly beard and looked in the direction Owen was looking. "Owen! That's Alfred, Lord Tennyson. He's one of the great Victorian English poets. He's reciting his poem, 'Ring Out, Wild Bells.'"

"Ah," said Owen. "So . . . not Santa."

"Wow. This is like a mini-museum, Patrick," said Alice, looking into a glass case positioned at the beginning of the display which held a pair of flintlock dueling pistols, an ax, and a set of brass knuckles, among other items. "I see the exhibit even covers crime in Victorian England, too. Is that a *harpoon*?"

"Yep," said Patrick proudly.

"Oh—and here's an article about Jack the Ripper," said Owen, peering into the glass case. "You ought to dig this stuff out again next Halloween."

Alice looked as well, first noticing a gleaming knife, which was positioned above a short article and a drawing of a shadowy figure. "That knife looks . . . very sharp," she said.

"It *is* very sharp," said Patrick, walking over to join them. "The actual one was a six-inch surgeon's knife. Jack the Ripper was probably the most notorious criminal of that age. But the more common crimes, as you can see, were things like robberies and petty thefts."

"Glad you have this case locked up tight, Patrick," said Sonny, tapping the glass over the knife.

"No worries," said Patrick, taking his keyring out of his pocket and jingling it. "The case is tempered glass, and this is the only key." He pointed further down in the display. "Be sure to take a look at the exhibit about food in Victorian England. That's my favorite part."

"Maybe it'll give us some insight into the whole *suet* thing," said Franny with a little shiver. "Suet scares me more than that knife."

They all laughed and stood visiting amiably about England and Christmas and the festival. Elmer Smallweed ambled up and joined them.

"Hello Mr. Smallweed—I mean, Elmer," said Alice.

"How nice to see you all," he said, nodding and smiling. He waved at Patrick, and Alice saw that he held a small black notebook in his hand. "Hello, Patrick. How about a hot cocoa in one of your Christmas mugs?"

Alice thought she noticed a slight shadow crossing Patrick's face as he nodded and went about opening another crate of commemorative mugs.

Elmer turned to Alice, Franny, and Owen and gave them a wink. "You know, even a healthy diet has some room for special indulgences like Patrick's outstanding hot cocoa."

Patrick wrapped Elmer's mug in a napkin and handed it to him. "Careful," he said. "It's really hot."

"Thank you kindly," said Elmer, giving Patrick a little bow. He tucked his notebook into his pocket and cupped the mug in both hands. "This warms the soul, doesn't it?" He smiled cordially at the whole group, then turned and walked back down Main Street whistling.

"What gives, Patrick?" Owen asked after Elmer had disappeared into the crowd.

Patrick took off his hat, ran a hand through his blond hair, and put his hat back on. "What do you mean?"

"How does Elmer score free drinks?"

Patrick frowned a little, but then smiled. "Elmer is an old friend of mine," he said. "A good friend. I owe him."

"That Elmer is a lucky guy," Owen said with a chuckle. "He has a lot of good friends in Blue Valley."

Taya Helms, the bartender at the Smiling Hound, came out with a fresh batch of hot cocoa. "Make way," she said coming up behind Patrick. "This is heavy."

"Huh?" Patrick turned around, accidentally knocking into Taya, who dropped the insulated pitcher, sending a cascade of hot chocolate all over Patrick's shoes and the ground around them.

"Oh, my gosh!" said Taya.

"Wow, that's hot!" said Patrick, stooping to pick up the pitcher.

"So sorry, Patrick."

"My fault," said Patrick, shaking his head. "I was distracted." He chuckled. "Good thing I'm wearing my waterproof boots. Hand me that rag, will you, Owen?"

A few minutes later, the mess was cleaned up and Taya was on her way back inside to make a fresh batch of hot cocoa. Alice, Owen, and Franny said their goodbyes, picked up their shopping bags, and headed home.

CHAPTER 6

The Holly and The Ivy Maze had been set up in a spot next to the lake that locals affectionately referred to as *The Clearing*. It was the site of jousts and balls every spring when the medieval faire came to town, and the perfect place for everything from summer picnics to Sunday strolls. It was just through the trees from Ben and Franny's house, and directly across the lake from the Cozy Bear Camp and Glamp.

The maze had been constructed using tall wooden frames which were completely covered in thick ivy and festive holly with red berries scattered throughout. It looked absolutely magical in the darkening night with flickering torches and candles all around, as well as twinkling lights strung from the trees overhead.

"Hey, isn't that Queen Victoria?" said Owen as they disembarked from the horse-drawn sleigh ride they'd taken from downtown. He waved at the costumed queen, who was just entering the maze. "Hey Vicky!" he called, and beamed when she looked back and graciously nodded. "Maybe this won't be so bad."

Just then, Chad Fender and his girlfriend Sadie Green came rushing out of the maze.

"I thought we'd never get out of there!" Chad was saying.

"That last ghost scared the life out of me," said Sadie.

"Um . . ." Owen stopped dead in his tracks.

Alice handed their tickets to Norman Mackenzie. "Everything going smoothly here tonight, Norman?" she asked.

"Great," said Norman, nodding and slinging an arm around his wife of three months, Pearl Ann. "Not one hitch—except people getting lost in there, of course. But that's sort of the point, isn't it?" he added with a chuckle.

"You gave us the best job at the festival, Alice. We're having so much fun," said Pearl Ann. "You should hear the shrieks of terror from inside when people come across that Ghost of Christmas Yet to Come!"

Alice glanced at Owen, who was still frozen to the same spot. "Glad you're having fun," she said to Pearl Ann. "And what happens—I mean, on the off chance that someone gets *really* lost in there?"

"In the middle of the maze, there's a raised platform," Norman explained. "If someone truly calls out for help, we go straight to that platform via our own special, secret short-cut, and then we can tell them exactly which way to turn to get out. You can see most of the maze from up there."

Alice took Owen's arm. "See, Owen? We can't get truly lost. Norman and Pearl Ann would come to our rescue if we needed them to."

"I still don't like the ghost factor," said Owen.

"Just keep telling yourself there are no real ghosts," said Franny, taking Owen's other arm and leading the three into the maze. "This is going to be fun," she said with a giggle.

Once inside, Alice was struck by how complex the maze actually was. There were countless twists and turns and everything looked the same, so that in the dim light, it was impossible to tell if you were backtracking or making progress. Before long, they were completely turned around. Fairly regularly, they'd pass another confounded group. They spotted Queen Victoria and Prince Albert. They caught sight of Sonny and Peyton. They saw Ethel Primrose from the Heritage Museum and Helen Hart from the library. They ran into Doc and Mrs. Howard who pointed to an upcoming corner and told them the Ghost of Christmas Past was just ahead.

Sure enough, the ghost, clad all in white, waited just around the corner, and handed them a sprig of holly. "I represent memory," the ghost said. "Cherish memories of the past, and let them connect you to who you were and still are."

"Will do," said Owen with a little shiver. "Let's go."

They wove on through the maze, passing a merry group of carolers who turned out to be the Gothic Trolls.

"They must be the most versatile musical group on the planet," said Alice.

The Gothic Trolls were comprised of lead singer and dulcimer player, Dante Johansen, along with Fenrir Larsen on the lute and Sía Olson at the harp. Normally, they'd be dressed in their signature medieval garb, entertaining the crowds at the Nottingham Faire that came to town every spring. But now, they'd been transformed, and strolled along in period costumes, singing classic holiday carols, their instruments left behind.

"You don't realize how amazing they are until you really hear them sing," said Franny.

The Trolls wished Alice, Owen, and Franny Merry Christmas, and then launched into "Here We Come A-Wassailing" as they moved on and disappeared around another corner.

"Let's go find the next ghost," said Alice, walking ahead.

"Wait for me," said Owen.

The Ghost of Christmas Present didn't take as long to locate. He was a big, jovial man, dressed in green, with a wreath on his head and a twinkle in his eyes. When they walked up to him, he bellowed, "Ah! So, you've found me! I am the Ghost of Christmas Present. Take this holly sprig, and remember that life is full of goodwill, joy, and blessing! Be of good cheer!"

Alice took the sprig, and they started down the path again. The Gothic Trolls were now doing a beautiful rendition of "The Holly and the Ivy" from somewhere in the maze. The woods around the maze smelled of pine, mingling with the crackling fires that burned further into the clearing, where festival goers could toast marshmallows and warm their hands. Alice found herself looking forward to standing next to one of those fires with a mug of spiced wine.

"Have any of you seen the Ghost of Christmas Yet to Come?" Patrick Sullivan caught up with them, a little out of breath. "He's the only one we have left to find." He glanced back at Marge Hartfield and Koi Butler, who he'd teamed up with.

"Us, too," said Alice. "We'll let you know if we see him."

"That is, if we can ever find you again," added Franny.

"How are candle sales going at the market, Marge?" asked Alice as they passed each other.

"Great! Almost sold out today. Koi and I are staying up late tonight to make more!"

"Okay, I'll admit it," said Owen as they wove on through the maze, out of breath and laughing. "This is fun."

"Where could that ghost be?" wondered Franny. "I feel like we've been through this maze a thousand times."

Owen, who'd confidently taken the lead, suddenly stopped, and Franny and Alice ran into him from behind.

"Owen, what's up?" said Franny.

"I think I found a secret passageway," said Owen. "Look! There's an opening in the wall! I'd be willing to bet that ghost is through here."

"Onward, fearless leader!" said Alice.

They pushed through the opening and came into yet another ivy-covered passageway that looked like all the rest, if not a little darker.

"Darn," said Owen. "No one here. I'm getting out my cell phone flashlight."

"No!" said Franny. "That's cheating."

"Go a little further," urged Alice. "I think the path cuts sharply to the right up there."

"How can you tell in all this darkness?" asked Franny.

They moved forward as one unit.

"I'm starting to feel spooky again," whispered Owen. "The Ghost of Christmas Yet to Come is all skeleton-y and ominous."

"Why is no one else down this way?" asked Alice. "Did we take a wrong turn?"

"Maybe this is—ow!" said Owen.

"Owen, what—ow!" said Alice, stumbling. "What *is* that?"

"What are you two talking about?" asked Franny, coming up last. But then she stumbled, too.

"Owen, get out your flashlight," said Alice, who had a very bad feeling in the pit of her stomach.

Owen quickly pulled out his cell phone and switched on the bright light. Once their eyes had adjusted, they were able to see that the dark mass on the ground at their feet was a person. A person who wasn't moving at all.

"Oh, my gosh!" cried Owen, dropping the cell phone.

There, lying on the ground with a very familiar knife sticking out of his chest, was Elmer Smallweed.

Alice felt sick as she squatted down and felt for a pulse, but found none. "He's dead."

Owen's shriek was so loud and so piercing that it wasn't long before others in the maze came running.

"Don't touch anything!" Alice warned as a small crowd began to gather. "Let's all move back a bit."

Owen had pulled himself together and dialed 9-1-1. "The

illion questions with no immediate
Ben, and Dewey came out and split
and contact information and running
f questions, trying to get an accurate
ere and when that night. One by one,
spective witnesses, warning them that
questions later.

g a small group in the cruiser and pulling
e wasn't able to identify them all, but was
an and Pearl Ann in the bunch, which
ey were probably the only two who had
son go into or out of the maze that night.

g a break in the chaos, hurried over to
standing and pulled her into his arms.
ow are you doing?"

up," Alice admitted. "But better than I
r ago, when we found Elmer." She felt a
d his name. "I still can't believe this

r gets any easier," said Luke, shaking his
ver stops surprising me—shocking me—that
ll another person."

he murder weapon," said Alice, almost in a

smiled. "Of course, you did. You notice every-
a hand to her cheek and sighed. "Dewey recog-
e'd been to the Victorian England exhibit at the
today. Whoever did this had a really sick sense

police are on the way," he said, and before long, sirens could be heard coming from town.

"Elmer's dead? This is crazy! We just saw him earlier today," said Patrick, who was standing next to Alice, out of breath from running. "Who would do this?"

"I'm not sure," Alice said slowly. "But do you still have the key to the case where the Victorian weapons are on display?"

"Of course, I do," said Patrick, confused. "I mean—not here with me." He paused. "Why are you looking at me like that, Alice?"

Alice swallowed hard, glancing over her shoulder to the passageway where Elmer lay. "The knife that killed Elmer. I think—I mean, I'm not positive, but I'm pretty sure it's Jack the Ripper's blade."

asking each other a m
answers. Finally, Luke,
up, taking down names
through an initial list
picture of who was w
they dismissed the pr
there might be further

Alice saw Dewey taki
out of the clearing. Sh
sure she'd seen Nor
made sense, since th
seen every single per

Ben and Lu
evening, were
area where the
Norman and P
the wooden pla
calling out whe
always agreeing

Luke, finally havi
where Alice was
"Now," he said. "H

"I'm pretty shake
was about an hou
pang as she sa
happened."

A little while later
Dewey, who had c
those festival goers
out and told to stay

"I know. It neve
head sadly. "It n
a person would

"This is a mess," Al
who were in there ca
wandered off."

"I recognized t
whisper.

"Let's go stand by the
might be here a while, a

"You did?" He
thing." He put
nized it too. H
Hound earlier

The fires in the cleari
huddled around them, ta

of style."

"Luke, there was an actor at the exhibit—a man I'd never met before. He was playing Alfred, Lord Tennyson. Maybe he broke into the case, took the knife, and snuck into the maze. He was standing right next to the exhibit all day."

"That was Dewey's first thought, too," said Luke. "But believe it or not, he already tracked the guy down. He's an actor by the name of Bob Sneed. But he has an alibi. He was doing an impromptu one-man show outside the Community Center when this evening's performance of *A Christmas Carol* let out. Multiple people saw him. I wish it had been that simple."

Alice felt her shoulders sink. "A murder investigation—nine days before our wedding."

Luke pulled Alice close and kissed the top of her head. "We're going to solve this thing before then. I'm sure of it."

"Let me know if we can help," said Alice, glancing over her shoulder to where Owen and Franny were standing talking to Ben.

"I'll say what I always say, Alice. Don't get involved. Stay safely out of the way." Luke looked at her and sighed. "But . . . if you do have any thoughts, please tell me."

Alice felt herself smiling again. "Because you know Owen, Franny, and I, when we put our heads together, are a crime-solving machine, right?"

"You have been known to crack a few," Luke admitted.

Ben gave him a little wave. "We'd better get over to the station. Dewey has everyone ready."

Luke smiled regretfully at Alice and joined Ben. "You three stay safe. We'll get home as soon as we can."

The Holly and the Ivy Maze was closed up for the rest of the evening, and festival goers who'd still been hanging around either caught one of the horse-drawn sleighs or began the short walk back to Main Street.

"Let's just walk," said Alice. "I could use the movement and fresh air."

"Agreed," said Owen, flipping on his cell phone's flashlight.

"Smells like rain," said Franny. "We'd better get a move on."

"Franny's nose is never wrong," said Owen. "Let's hit the road."

Alice felt a sense of relief and a surge of energy when they turned from Phlox onto Main, and the whole street was still cheerily decorated and ablaze with Christmas lights.

"Let's go to my apartment and snuggle up to wait for Luke and Ben to get home tonight," said Alice. "We can watch one of our comfort movies."

"Great idea," said Owen. "It's not like I could sleep anyway."

"We can break out some of the healthy snacks we bought yesterday," said Franny.

"Yes!" agreed Owen. "Those matcha-cocoa cupcakes are calling my name."

The wind suddenly picked up and gusted down the street, blowing ornaments and tinsel off of trees, and causing twinkle lights and garlands to flap about wildly.

"The cold front's blowing in," said Alice. "We're going to have a mess to clean up in the morning."

"Hurry. Let's get inside," said Owen, picking up the pace.

But Alice's steps slowed as they passed the Christmas Hound.

"Come on, Alice! It's getting cold!" said Owen. "And even I can smell the rain now."

But Alice stopped walking. "The glass case where the knife was," she said, pointing. "It's standing wide open."

CHAPTER 8

"Remind me why we decided to watch *Krampus's Holiday of Horror*," said Owen, snuggling a little deeper down into Alice's couch and pulling her patchwork quilt up high enough that he could barely see over it.

"Because we wanted to be scared out of our wits?" suggested Franny.

"Because we weren't already spooked enough?" said Alice. "Franny, hand me another one of those cupcakes."

"I'm pretty sure we were going to start cutting back on the sweets," said Owen, taking a big bite of a cupcake.

"We'll start that tomorrow," said Alice, petting Poppy, who had just contentedly curled up between her and Owen. "We tripped over a dead body tonight, and I am in desperate need of chocolate."

As if on cue, thunder clapped outside, and the first drops of rain began to fall.

"Who do you think would kill Elmer Smallweed?" Franny wondered. "He seemed like such a nice man."

"I can't even begin to guess," said Alice. "But I'm worried about Patrick."

"Because the murder weapon was part of his collection of strange artifacts," said Owen, nodding.

"And because he had the only key to the case that knife was in—and you saw the case when we walked by. It hadn't been broken into. It had been unlocked."

"So, either someone took the key—" Franny said.

"Or Patrick killed Elmer Smallweed," said Owen.

There was a bright flash of lightning outside and the thunder crashed again.

"What's that banging sound?" asked Owen.

"Um, thunder?" said Alice.

"Not that. Listen."

Alice paused the movie and they all sat quietly huddled together for a moment. Sure enough, there was a banging noise coming from downstairs. Poppy's ears perked up and she stood, now on high alert.

"See? Poppy hears it too," whispered Owen.

"Holy cow, it's Krampus!" said Franny, pulling the quilt entirely over her head.

"It's probably just Ben and Luke," said Alice, trying to keep the tremor out of her voice.

"But they have a key to the building," said Owen. "Why would they be banging around down there?"

The banging sounded yet again.

"I'm not going down there," said Owen.

"I'm not either," said Franny.

Alice thought for a moment. "One of us should run out into the garden and look down to see if someone's down there."

"Good idea," said Owen. "Which one of us?"

"I'll go, but not by myself," said Franny.

"Alice, get that giant umbrella you have. We'll go together," said Owen.

"Fine, but only to prove there's no one there," said Alice, jumping up and hurrying to her coat closet. She returned with a huge umbrella. "You made fun of me when I got this," she said, popping up the umbrella. "But who's laughing now?"

They all got under the umbrella, and together they flung open Alice's French doors and scurried out into the downpour.

"Can you see anyone?" asked Owen as they leaned over the façade and strained to see the sidewalk below.

"It's so dark, it's—" Alice's words were cut off as a huge bolt of lightning illuminated the street. And there, standing at the door of The Paper Owl, looking up at them with wild eyes in the flashing light, was Patrick Sullivan.

CHAPTER 9

They only hesitated a moment before running downstairs and letting a shivering, dripping-wet Patrick into The Paper Owl.

"I'm in big trouble! I need help!" Patrick said, his voice sounding shaky and panicked.

"I'll run upstairs and get you some dry sweats to change into," said Owen.

"And I'll get the coffee started," said Franny, leading Patrick through the cased opening from the bookstore into Joe's.

Within a few minutes, a much calmer Patrick was warm and dry and cupping a steaming mug of coffee in his hands. "I don't know what I'm going to do," he said. "I need your help."

"What's going on?" asked Alice, shivering a little as the memory of the open glass case crossed her thoughts. "I assume this is about Elmer's death."

"Yes," said Patrick. "I just came from the police station. I was questioned extensively. I mean, they asked me the same questions again and again until I thought my head would explode. I kept thinking surely they couldn't think *I* killed Elmer Smallweed. But you saw the murder weapon. It belonged to me. It has my finger prints all over it. And sure, I was right there in the maze where it happened. I'm telling you I did *not* kill the man, but I know I'm the prime suspect. The police didn't have the evidence to keep me there, but they've told me not to go far."

"But Patrick, it defies logic that you'd kill Elmer," said Alice. "I mean, you'd need a motive. And you don't have one."

There was a long pause.

Owen cleared his throat. "You didn't have a motive to rid the world of Elmer Smallweed, did you, Patrick?" he asked gently.

Patrick looked at Owen, then Franny, then Alice. "I did have a reason to wish him dead and gone," he finally said.

"Can you tell us what that is?" asked Alice.

Patrick hesitated for a moment longer, then seemed to resolve within himself that it was time to come clean. "Elmer Smallweed had been blackmailing me. He knew . . . something about me that, if it were to be made public, would ruin me. And he's been holding it over my head for years."

"So that's why he never paid for drinks," said Owen.

"That's right," said Patrick. "All of Smallweed's drinks were free. His food was free. And worse, he demanded money. When he'd come around waving that little black book of his, that meant it was payday." Patrick sighed deeply. "I'd pass him the cash in a cocktail napkin or some such."

"That happened today!" said Alice, straightening. "I remember the black notebook, and I remember the napkin you wrapped around his mug of cocoa."

"That notebook was where he kept his list of the payments I was making," said Patrick. "It was always a bad day when he showed up with that."

"I remember him not paying for his cocoa," added Owen. "That scoundrel!"

"He was a scoundrel," Patrick agreed. "But I was powerless to stop him."

"But what did he have on you, Patrick?" asked Franny. "You're not the kind of person to avoid a fight. It must've been something terrible for you to let him get away with blackmail."

Patrick hesitated again, but finally spoke. "This is something that's weighed on me for more years than I'd care to admit. You see, I came to this country from Ireland about twenty-five years ago, when I was, oh, eighteen years old, I guess. I came here on a student visa, with a full scholarship to study history at Rhodes College in Memphis." He paused and took a long sip of coffee. "I fell in love with this place—with this country, this state, the Smoky Mountains . . ." He gazed toward the windows at the front of the coffee shop, where the lightening still flashed and the rain ran steadily down the glass panes. "And then I found Blue Valley." He smiled. "And I knew I'd found my home."

"I felt the same way the first time I came here," said Owen. "It instantly felt like home, and pretty soon, these two became my family." He tilted his head toward Alice and Franny.

"Exactly so," said Patrick, nodding. "I was dating a girl at the time who lived up in Runesville. We visited her family once, and drove through Blue Valley. We stopped at Whitman's grocery store to buy snacks. I looked down Main Street. I saw the park. I just knew I belonged here. I wanted to open my own pub one day, and this . . ." He got up and walked to the windows and looked up Main toward the Smiling Hound. "This was the place to do it. I knew it in my gut." He turned back to Alice, Owen, and Franny. "I decided to stay. My, uh, girlfriend agreed to marry me so that I could get a green card."

"What ever became of her?" asked Alice.

"No idea. Like I said, she comes from Runesville. She had a lot of family there—maybe she even still lives there. But we were just kids. We got in an argument over some silly thing I can't even remember, and we broke up. I never heard from her again. And I . . . well, I should've been the one to call her, but my stubborn pride got in the way, and then eventually, so much time had passed that I thought it was too late. It *is* too late. But technically, I am still married. And somehow, Elmer found that out. I mean, my wife and I never even lived together. I could be deported and she could be in trouble if anyone found out."

"And you didn't tell this to Luke or Ben?" asked Franny.

"They're honorable men," said Patrick, shaking his head. "They'd have to do the right thing and report me to the authorities if they knew. But they'll find out soon enough and I'll be tried for murder *and* deported in one go, I guess." He came back to the table and sat down and looked at them. "I know it's a lot to ask, but you three have solved mysteries before. Please. I need your help."

"Ben is my husband," said Franny. "And Alice's brother. And Luke is Alice's fiancé and our dear friend. You're asking us to keep this from them?"

"No. I mean, only for a little while," said Patrick, holding up his hands. "You have my word I'll tell them everything if the killer isn't caught within a couple days. I just hoped that in not telling them my story, I could buy a little time for the killer to come to light. I'm just asking you to help that process along."

"What's your wife's name?" asked Alice. When Patrick hesitated to answer, Alice insisted. "Patrick, if you're asking us to help you, you're going to have to trust us."

"But by now, she's probably forgotten about me. Maybe she even figured a way to marry someone else. I don't want to make things hard for her." He sighed. "Truth is, I've never gotten over her green eyes or her shiny hair or her sweet smile. And I wouldn't want to hurt her any more than I already have."

When this was met with Alice's stoniest gaze, Patrick shook his head. "Okay, okay." He swallowed. "Sophie. Sophie Sullivan. Her maiden name was O'Toole." He chuckled. "We met at university, on St. Patrick's Day, freshman year."

Alice, Owen, and Franny looked at one another and tiny nods were exchanged as they made an unspoken agreement.

"We'll try our best to help you," said Alice. "But if we can't solve this thing within two days, you have to go back to the police and tell them the whole truth, Patrick. Because if they find this out on their own, it'll only make you appear even more guilty."

Patrick breathed a sigh of relief. "I know," he said. "You have my word. Thank you."

They gave Patrick hugs and let him borrow Alice's giant umbrella.

"Please be careful though," he said, turning back before opening the door to leave. "Somewhere out there, a killer is still on the loose."

CHAPTER 10

After a restless night, where even Poppy left the bed in a feline huff due to all the tossing and turning, Alice got up and went into the bathroom. She was shocked by the level of puffiness her eyes had attained, and decided to take a hot shower before meeting up with Owen and Franny.

By the time she emerged onto the rooftop garden, she felt refreshed and clean, if still a bit tired. The storm from the night before had cleared the air, which was now cold and crisp and perfectly wintery. Franny and Owen were dragging a little bit themselves after their late night, but Franny had brought up a carafe of her industrial-strength breakfast blend, and Owen had brought a box up from Sourdough.

"A new experimental recipe," he said. "Hilda and I have been trying out healthy alternatives. These—" He opened the box with a flourish. "—are our cinnamon swirl, whole-grain breakfast buns. Guaranteed to set you right."

"Delicious!" said Franny, taking a bite of a warm bun.

"Now that we're all awake, let's talk about Patrick's situation," said Alice.

"Did you notice how his eyes sparkled when he was talking about his wife Sophie?" said Franny.

"Yep," said Owen. "He's got it pretty bad, even after all these years. How romantic is that?"

"I think we should try to get in touch with her," said Alice.

"I can call my cousin Sara," said Franny. "Maybe she knows Sophie."

"Oh, that's right. I'd forgotten you have a cousin in Runesville," said Alice. "Please do that. It's a tiny town. Odds are, she's at least heard of the O'Toole family."

"Meanwhile, do we definitely believe that Patrick didn't kill Elmer?" asked Owen.

"He had means, motive, and opportunity," said Alice. "But Patrick's no killer. I remember when he moved here and opened the Hound. We've known him ever since. He's always been the same decent man."

"I remember, too," said Franny, nodding. "Right from the start, the Smiling Hound was the place to be."

"So, what we need to do is to figure out who else would want to kill Elmer Smallweed," said Alice. "And then start looking at whether they were at the maze when Elmer was killed and whether they have alibis."

"I've got it! Faith Lindor!" said Owen, sloshing his coffee in his excitement.

police are on the way," he said, and before long, sirens could be heard coming from town.

"Elmer's dead? This is crazy! We just saw him earlier today," said Patrick, who was standing next to Alice, out of breath from running. "Who would do this?"

"I'm not sure," Alice said slowly. "But do you still have the key to the case where the Victorian weapons are on display?"

"Of course, I do," said Patrick, confused. "I mean—not here with me." He paused. "Why are you looking at me like that, Alice?"

Alice swallowed hard, glancing over her shoulder to the passageway where Elmer lay. "The knife that killed Elmer. I think—I mean, I'm not positive, but I'm pretty sure it's Jack the Ripper's blade."

CHAPTER 7

Ben and Luke, who had been patrolling the clearing that evening, were the first to arrive at the maze. They found the area where the body lay with the help of the Gothic Trolls and Norman and Pearl Ann, who were by then all standing up on the wooden platform at the center of the maze, exuberantly calling out when and where to turn—and not necessarily always agreeing on the best route.

A little while later, paramedics were led in, along with Officer Dewey, who had come from the station, and at the same time, those festival goers who were still in the maze were directed out and told to stay put for the time being.

"This is a mess," Alice heard Norman say. "A lot of the folks who were in there came out on their own and have already wandered off."

"Let's go stand by the fire and warm up," said Alice. "We might be here a while, and I suddenly feel very cold."

The fires in the clearing were stoked up, and everyone huddled around them, talking about what had happened and asking each other a million questions with no immediate answers. Finally, Luke, Ben, and Dewey came out and split up, taking down names and contact information and running through an initial list of questions, trying to get an accurate picture of who was where and when that night. One by one, they dismissed the prospective witnesses, warning them that there might be further questions later.

Alice saw Dewey taking a small group in the cruiser and pulling out of the clearing. She wasn't able to identify them all, but was sure she'd seen Norman and Pearl Ann in the bunch, which made sense, since they were probably the only two who had seen every single person go into or out of the maze that night.

Luke, finally having a break in the chaos, hurried over to where Alice was standing and pulled her into his arms. "Now," he said. "How are you doing?"

"I'm pretty shaken up," Alice admitted. "But better than I was about an hour ago, when we found Elmer." She felt a pang as she said his name. "I still can't believe this happened."

"I know. It never gets any easier," said Luke, shaking his head sadly. "It never stops surprising me—shocking me—that a person would kill another person."

"I recognized the murder weapon," said Alice, almost in a whisper.

"You did?" He smiled. "Of course, you did. You notice everything." He put a hand to her cheek and sighed. "Dewey recognized it too. He'd been to the Victorian England exhibit at the Hound earlier today. Whoever did this had a really sick sense of style."

"Luke, there was an actor at the exhibit—a man I'd never met before. He was playing Alfred, Lord Tennyson. Maybe he broke into the case, took the knife, and snuck into the maze. He was standing right next to the exhibit all day."

"That was Dewey's first thought, too," said Luke. "But believe it or not, he already tracked the guy down. He's an actor by the name of Bob Sneed. But he has an alibi. He was doing an impromptu one-man show outside the Community Center when this evening's performance of *A Christmas Carol* let out. Multiple people saw him. I wish it had been that simple."

Alice felt her shoulders sink. "A murder investigation—nine days before our wedding."

Luke pulled Alice close and kissed the top of her head. "We're going to solve this thing before then. I'm sure of it."

"Let me know if we can help," said Alice, glancing over her shoulder to where Owen and Franny were standing talking to Ben.

"I'll say what I always say, Alice. Don't get involved. Stay safely out of the way." Luke looked at her and sighed. "But . . . if you do have any thoughts, please tell me."

Alice felt herself smiling again. "Because you know Owen, Franny, and I, when we put our heads together, are a crime-solving machine, right?"

"You have been known to crack a few," Luke admitted.

Ben gave him a little wave. "We'd better get over to the station. Dewey has everyone ready."

Luke smiled regretfully at Alice and joined Ben. "You three stay safe. We'll get home as soon as we can."

The Holly and the Ivy Maze was closed up for the rest of the evening, and festival goers who'd still been hanging around either caught one of the horse-drawn sleighs or began the short walk back to Main Street.

"Let's just walk," said Alice. "I could use the movement and fresh air."

"Agreed," said Owen, flipping on his cell phone's flashlight.

"Smells like rain," said Franny. "We'd better get a move on."

"Franny's nose is never wrong," said Owen. "Let's hit the road."

Alice felt a sense of relief and a surge of energy when they turned from Phlox onto Main, and the whole street was still cheerily decorated and ablaze with Christmas lights.

"Let's go to my apartment and snuggle up to wait for Luke and Ben to get home tonight," said Alice. "We can watch one of our comfort movies."

"Great idea," said Owen. "It's not like I could sleep anyway."

"We can break out some of the healthy snacks we bought yesterday," said Franny.

"Yes!" agreed Owen. "Those matcha-cocoa cupcakes are calling my name."

The wind suddenly picked up and gusted down the street, blowing ornaments and tinsel off of trees, and causing twinkle lights and garlands to flap about wildly.

"The cold front's blowing in," said Alice. "We're going to have a mess to clean up in the morning."

"Hurry. Let's get inside," said Owen, picking up the pace.

But Alice's steps slowed as they passed the Christmas Hound.

"Come on, Alice! It's getting cold!" said Owen. "And even I can smell the rain now."

But Alice stopped walking. "The glass case where the knife was," she said, pointing. "It's standing wide open."

CHAPTER 8

"Remind me why we decided to watch *Krampus's Holiday of Horror*," said Owen, snuggling a little deeper down into Alice's couch and pulling her patchwork quilt up high enough that he could barely see over it.

"Because we wanted to be scared out of our wits?" suggested Franny.

"Because we weren't already spooked enough?" said Alice. "Franny, hand me another one of those cupcakes."

"I'm pretty sure we were going to start cutting back on the sweets," said Owen, taking a big bite of a cupcake.

"We'll start that tomorrow," said Alice, petting Poppy, who had just contentedly curled up between her and Owen. "We tripped over a dead body tonight, and I am in desperate need of chocolate."

As if on cue, thunder clapped outside, and the first drops of rain began to fall.

"Who do you think would kill Elmer Smallweed?" Franny wondered. "He seemed like such a nice man."

"I can't even begin to guess," said Alice. "But I'm worried about Patrick."

"Because the murder weapon was part of his collection of strange artifacts," said Owen, nodding.

"And because he had the only key to the case that knife was in—and you saw the case when we walked by. It hadn't been broken into. It had been unlocked."

"So, either someone took the key—" Franny said.

"Or Patrick killed Elmer Smallweed," said Owen.

There was a bright flash of lightning outside and the thunder crashed again.

"What's that banging sound?" asked Owen.

"Um, thunder?" said Alice.

"Not that. Listen."

Alice paused the movie and they all sat quietly huddled together for a moment. Sure enough, there was a banging noise coming from downstairs. Poppy's ears perked up and she stood, now on high alert.

"See? Poppy hears it too," whispered Owen.

"Holy cow, it's Krampus!" said Franny, pulling the quilt entirely over her head.

"It's probably just Ben and Luke," said Alice, trying to keep the tremor out of her voice.

"But they have a key to the building," said Owen. "Why would they be banging around down there?"

The banging sounded yet again.

"I'm not going down there," said Owen.

"I'm not either," said Franny.

Alice thought for a moment. "One of us should run out into the garden and look down to see if someone's down there."

"Good idea," said Owen. "Which one of us?"

"I'll go, but not by myself," said Franny.

"Alice, get that giant umbrella you have. We'll go together," said Owen.

"Fine, but only to prove there's no one there," said Alice, jumping up and hurrying to her coat closet. She returned with a huge umbrella. "You made fun of me when I got this," she said, popping up the umbrella. "But who's laughing now?"

They all got under the umbrella, and together they flung open Alice's French doors and scurried out into the downpour.

"Can you see anyone?" asked Owen as they leaned over the façade and strained to see the sidewalk below.

"It's so dark, it's—" Alice's words were cut off as a huge bolt of lightning illuminated the street. And there, standing at the door of The Paper Owl, looking up at them with wild eyes in the flashing light, was Patrick Sullivan.

CHAPTER 9

They only hesitated a moment before running downstairs and letting a shivering, dripping-wet Patrick into The Paper Owl.

"I'm in big trouble! I need help!" Patrick said, his voice sounding shaky and panicked.

"I'll run upstairs and get you some dry sweats to change into," said Owen.

"And I'll get the coffee started," said Franny, leading Patrick through the cased opening from the bookstore into Joe's.

Within a few minutes, a much calmer Patrick was warm and dry and cupping a steaming mug of coffee in his hands. "I don't know what I'm going to do," he said. "I need your help."

"What's going on?" asked Alice, shivering a little as the memory of the open glass case crossed her thoughts. "I assume this is about Elmer's death."

"Yes," said Patrick. "I just came from the police station. I was questioned extensively. I mean, they asked me the same questions again and again until I thought my head would explode. I kept thinking surely they couldn't think *I* killed Elmer Smallweed. But you saw the murder weapon. It belonged to me. It has my finger prints all over it. And sure, I was right there in the maze where it happened. I'm telling you I did *not* kill the man, but I know I'm the prime suspect. The police didn't have the evidence to keep me there, but they've told me not to go far."

"But Patrick, it defies logic that you'd kill Elmer," said Alice. "I mean, you'd need a motive. And you don't have one."

There was a long pause.

Owen cleared his throat. "You didn't have a motive to rid the world of Elmer Smallweed, did you, Patrick?" he asked gently.

Patrick looked at Owen, then Franny, then Alice. "I did have a reason to wish him dead and gone," he finally said.

"Can you tell us what that is?" asked Alice.

Patrick hesitated for a moment longer, then seemed to resolve within himself that it was time to come clean. "Elmer Smallweed had been blackmailing me. He knew . . . something about me that, if it were to be made public, would ruin me. And he's been holding it over my head for years."

"So that's why he never paid for drinks," said Owen.

"That's right," said Patrick. "All of Smallweed's drinks were free. His food was free. And worse, he demanded money. When he'd come around waving that little black book of his, that meant it was payday." Patrick sighed deeply. "I'd pass him the cash in a cocktail napkin or some such."

"That happened today!" said Alice, straightening. "I remember the black notebook, and I remember the napkin you wrapped around his mug of cocoa."

"That notebook was where he kept his list of the payments I was making," said Patrick. "It was always a bad day when he showed up with that."

"I remember him not paying for his cocoa," added Owen. "That scoundrel!"

"He was a scoundrel," Patrick agreed. "But I was powerless to stop him."

"But what did he have on you, Patrick?" asked Franny. "You're not the kind of person to avoid a fight. It must've been something terrible for you to let him get away with blackmail."

Patrick hesitated again, but finally spoke. "This is something that's weighed on me for more years than I'd care to admit. You see, I came to this country from Ireland about twenty-five years ago, when I was, oh, eighteen years old, I guess. I came here on a student visa, with a full scholarship to study history at Rhodes College in Memphis." He paused and took a long sip of coffee. "I fell in love with this place—with this country, this state, the Smoky Mountains . . ." He gazed toward the windows at the front of the coffee shop, where the lightening still flashed and the rain ran steadily down the glass panes. "And then I found Blue Valley." He smiled. "And I knew I'd found my home."

"I felt the same way the first time I came here," said Owen. "It instantly felt like home, and pretty soon, these two became my family." He tilted his head toward Alice and Franny.

"Exactly so," said Patrick, nodding. "I was dating a girl at the time who lived up in Runesville. We visited her family once, and drove through Blue Valley. We stopped at Whitman's grocery store to buy snacks. I looked down Main Street. I saw the park. I just knew I belonged here. I wanted to open my own pub one day, and this . . ." He got up and walked to the windows and looked up Main toward the Smiling Hound. "This was the place to do it. I knew it in my gut." He turned back to Alice, Owen, and Franny. "I decided to stay. My, uh, girlfriend agreed to marry me so that I could get a green card."

"What ever became of her?" asked Alice.

"No idea. Like I said, she comes from Runesville. She had a lot of family there—maybe she even still lives there. But we were just kids. We got in an argument over some silly thing I can't even remember, and we broke up. I never heard from her again. And I . . . well, I should've been the one to call her, but my stubborn pride got in the way, and then eventually, so much time had passed that I thought it was too late. It *is* too late. But technically, I am still married. And somehow, Elmer found that out. I mean, my wife and I never even lived together. I could be deported and she could be in trouble if anyone found out."

"And you didn't tell this to Luke or Ben?" asked Franny.

"They're honorable men," said Patrick, shaking his head. "They'd have to do the right thing and report me to the authorities if they knew. But they'll find out soon enough and I'll be tried for murder *and* deported in one go, I guess." He came back to the table and sat down and looked at them. "I know it's a lot to ask, but you three have solved mysteries before. Please. I need your help."

"Ben is my husband," said Franny. "And Alice's brother. And Luke is Alice's fiancé and our dear friend. You're asking us to keep this from them?"

"No. I mean, only for a little while," said Patrick, holding up his hands. "You have my word I'll tell them everything if the killer isn't caught within a couple days. I just hoped that in not telling them my story, I could buy a little time for the killer to come to light. I'm just asking you to help that process along."

"What's your wife's name?" asked Alice. When Patrick hesitated to answer, Alice insisted. "Patrick, if you're asking us to help you, you're going to have to trust us."

"But by now, she's probably forgotten about me. Maybe she even figured a way to marry someone else. I don't want to make things hard for her." He sighed. "Truth is, I've never gotten over her green eyes or her shiny hair or her sweet smile. And I wouldn't want to hurt her any more than I already have."

When this was met with Alice's stoniest gaze, Patrick shook his head. "Okay, okay." He swallowed. "Sophie. Sophie Sullivan. Her maiden name was O'Toole." He chuckled. "We met at university, on St. Patrick's Day, freshman year."

Alice, Owen, and Franny looked at one another and tiny nods were exchanged as they made an unspoken agreement.

"We'll try our best to help you," said Alice. "But if we can't solve this thing within two days, you have to go back to the police and tell them the whole truth, Patrick. Because if they find this out on their own, it'll only make you appear even more guilty."

Patrick breathed a sigh of relief. "I know," he said. "You have my word. Thank you."

They gave Patrick hugs and let him borrow Alice's giant umbrella.

"Please be careful though," he said, turning back before opening the door to leave. "Somewhere out there, a killer is still on the loose."

CHAPTER 10

After a restless night, where even Poppy left the bed in a feline huff due to all the tossing and turning, Alice got up and went into the bathroom. She was shocked by the level of puffiness her eyes had attained, and decided to take a hot shower before meeting up with Owen and Franny.

By the time she emerged onto the rooftop garden, she felt refreshed and clean, if still a bit tired. The storm from the night before had cleared the air, which was now cold and crisp and perfectly wintery. Franny and Owen were dragging a little bit themselves after their late night, but Franny had brought up a carafe of her industrial-strength breakfast blend, and Owen had brought a box up from Sourdough.

"A new experimental recipe," he said. "Hilda and I have been trying out healthy alternatives. These—" He opened the box with a flourish. "—are our cinnamon swirl, whole-grain breakfast buns. Guaranteed to set you right."

"Delicious!" said Franny, taking a bite of a warm bun.

"Now that we're all awake, let's talk about Patrick's situation," said Alice.

"Did you notice how his eyes sparkled when he was talking about his wife Sophie?" said Franny.

"Yep," said Owen. "He's got it pretty bad, even after all these years. How romantic is that?"

"I think we should try to get in touch with her," said Alice.

"I can call my cousin Sara," said Franny. "Maybe she knows Sophie."

"Oh, that's right. I'd forgotten you have a cousin in Runesville," said Alice. "Please do that. It's a tiny town. Odds are, she's at least heard of the O'Toole family."

"Meanwhile, do we definitely believe that Patrick didn't kill Elmer?" asked Owen.

"He had means, motive, and opportunity," said Alice. "But Patrick's no killer. I remember when he moved here and opened the Hound. We've known him ever since. He's always been the same decent man."

"I remember, too," said Franny, nodding. "Right from the start, the Smiling Hound was the place to be."

"So, what we need to do is to figure out who else would want to kill Elmer Smallweed," said Alice. "And then start looking at whether they were at the maze when Elmer was killed and whether they have alibis."

"I've got it! Faith Lindor!" said Owen, sloshing his coffee in his excitement.

"Faith?" asked Franny. "She's an even less likely killer than Patrick."

"That's not what I mean," said Owen. "Faith has been giving Elmer free stuff from Crumpets for ages. I've seen her do it. Maybe he was blackmailing more people than just Patrick."

"You're right," said Alice. "We need to look into all of Elmer's so-called *friends*. Maybe they were really his victims. And that certainly could be motive to get rid of him."

"So, we know he was blackmailing Patrick. And we think he might've been after Faith, too. Who else?" wondered Franny.

"Who knows," said Owen. "Most people who are being blackmailed aren't really excited about revealing it. It's not as though we can put an ad in the *Blue Valley Post* alongside a picture of Elmer. *Have you been blackmailed by this man?*"

"The notebook!" said Alice. "The little black notebook Elmer carried. Patrick said that's where Elmer kept a record of his payments. We need to find it. Let's call Patrick right now and see if he has any idea where Elmer kept it."

Alice called Patrick's cell phone, and he picked up immediately.

"Oh, yes, I know right where he kept it," said Patrick. "I was forced to go into his stupid vitamin shop last week, since it was my job to distribute the window posters to all the downtown businesses for the festival. He had the notebook out on the counter, and shoved it into a hidden drawer when I walked in, but I saw where he put it. I thought about destroying it myself if I could lay my hands on it, but he never left the room."

Patrick told Alice that he'd seen Elmer put the notebook into a drawer under the cash register at the front counter. When Patrick had casually peered around the counter while Elmer was hanging the festival poster in the window, he'd seen that there was no visible drawer there. "It was one of those hidden panels is my best guess," said Patrick. "There were other drawers to the left, but the hidden one is directly under the register. No doubt that shyster kept that notebook where no one could stumble across it."

"Let's stroll over to The Daily Dose right now," said Alice after she'd hung up with Patrick. "I'm sure the Kingsleys are keeping the place open. We can do a little snooping around."

"We'll need a brilliant diversion to get whichever Kingsley that's working there to look the other way," said Owen. "We can plan it out on the way."

By the time they'd reached The Daily Dose, they'd hatched a simple scheme. They pulled open the glass door and stepped inside to find the shop empty except for Sonny, who was unloading a box of protein powder and setting it on a shelf.

"Hello," he said brightly. "Welcome in."

"Glad to see the shop is open," said Alice. "We were afraid it might be closed, what with Elmer . . ."

Sonny nodded. "Peyton and I are going to run the shop for now. She's holding down the fort next door, and I'm looking after things here. The Daily Dose really compliments what we do at the Good Earth Emporium anyway, and Elmer would've wanted his vision to be realized. We'll work out the formalities later, of course. But for now, we're keeping the doors open and hoping for the best."

"That's wonderful," said Franny.

"What can I help you find today?" asked Sonny.

"Franny and I wanted to have another look at the Nutrique line," said Alice. "Elmer told us a little bit about it when we were here two days ago, but could you show us the different products?"

"Sure," said Sonny. "Those are top of the line—Elmer's own formulations." He hurried over and began discussing each product in the Nutrique family, and Alice and Franny nodded and asked lots of questions.

A moment later, there was a loud crash from behind.

"Oh, my gosh! I'm so sorry!" said Owen, who was now standing next to a huge pile of vitamins, which were scattered all over the floor. "I was trying to make a good guess about how many vitamins were in the jar . . ."

"What happened to the lid?" asked Sonny, rushing over.

"I guess it was loose," said Owen, throwing up his hands and looking genuinely shocked. "Here, let me help clean these up."

"I'll go get a broom—"

"I think it'll go really fast if I hold the jar while you sort of just scoop them in with your hands," said Owen, kneeling on the floor. "Ow! Be careful when you kneel down. These things are like little rocks stabbing your knees."

Owen rattled on, keeping Sonny fully engaged, while Alice and Franny hurried silently over to the counter, where they searched for the hidden drawer. Every time Sonny started to turn around, Owen would think of another pressing question to ask him about health food, vitamins, or fitness. Sure enough, as Patrick had said, there was no drawer visible directly under the cash register. It just looked like a wooden panel that matched the rest of the counter. Alice gave Owen a bewildered look, which he returned with a 'hurry up!' look of his own. She felt around for any kind of latch or crack, but found only the paper-fine seam of wood meeting wood. Finally, just as the last of the vitamins were almost cleared from the floor, Alice pressed against the panel and breathed a sigh of relief when it quietly snapped open.

As Patrick had predicted, the black notebook lay within, along with a few bundles of cash. Alice grabbed the notebook and stuffed in into her coat pocket while Franny closed the drawer quietly. Then the two of them hurried over to the nearest shelf and pretended to be deeply engrossed, studying a display of superfood supplements as Sonny finally lifted the heavy jar and set it on its pedestal, after checking that the lid was screwed on very tightly.

"Why didn't you help us pick up the vitamins?" Owen scolded in a convincingly exasperated tone. He turned to Sonny. "These two." He rolled his eyes. "They are *so* into healthy living."

"Oh, boy. We'd better get going," said Franny. "My mom is dropping Theo at the coffee shop. They should be done with their morning stroll right about now."

They took a few more brochures about Nutrique, thanked Sonny for his time, and left the shop with Owen still profusely apologizing for spilling the vitamins.

"That was close," said Alice, feeling more relieved the further they got down the street. She reached into her coat pocket and felt the notebook inside, trying not to think about the fact that it belonged to a dead man. "Let's get home and see what was so important to Elmer that he went to such great lengths to keep this thing hidden."

Owen nodded. "And so dangerous that it might've gotten him killed."

CHAPTER 11

After checking to make sure things were running smoothly in their shops, Alice, Owen, and Franny reconvened at the café table in the garden—along with baby Theo who didn't have a lot to contribute to the discussion because he was sound asleep after his walk with Granny Brown.

Alice took out the notebook and opened it on the table.

"Jackpot!" said Owen. "It's a list of names." He took a closer look and pointed at the page. "And *that* confirms why Faith was giving Elmer free scones."

Faith Lindor was the first name on Elmer's list, followed by Patrick Sullivan, Arnold Zwicke, and Sonny and Peyton Kingsley.

"Looks like Elmer had been into Faith the longest," said Alice, looking over the neatly written list of dates and payments.

"Seems like Elmer was surprisingly well organized for a blackmailing criminal," said Owen.

"It makes me sick that these people—all of whom are friends of ours—have been silently carrying this burden around," said Franny.

"No wonder someone killed the guy," said Owen.

"Someone had finally had enough," agreed Alice.

"We have to show this to Ben and Luke," said Franny.

"We will," said Alice. "Very soon. We'll all be together tonight when they get home from work. We can tell them then." A slow smile spread across her face. "But wouldn't it be even nicer if we had *more* information to share by then? I mean, we have the day off. What if we spend it going through the people on this list—talking to them, feeling them out, checking for alibis. We know almost exactly when Elmer was killed, because we were there."

Owen clapped. "Ladies—and baby—" he pointed at the snoozing Theo, "the game is on! Where do we start?"

Alice closed the notebook. "We start by finding out who on this list was in the maze when Elmer was killed."

As they walked down Main Street, pushing Theo in his stroller, they passed the Gothic Trolls, who were making the rounds, singing carols. They saw Queen Victoria and Prince Albert posing for photos with festival goers. They saw a large crowd gathered at the Christmas Hound, sipping cocoa from commemorative mugs and walking through the Victorian England history exhibit—minus Jack the Ripper's knife. Trinkets, the souvenir and ice cream shop had drawn quite a crowd with its special holiday treats, including a Make Your Own Snow Ice Cream class, where children were gathered around a table that had been set outside, and were stirring sugar and vanilla into shaved ice.

When they got to Crumpets, they went right inside, and were greeted by a warm waft of wonderful aromas.

"Cinnamon," said Franny, sniffing the air. "And nutmeg."

"That's my holiday eggnog cream scones you smell," said Faith Lindor with a smile.

"Sounds delicious," said Alice. "We'll take half a dozen."

While Faith bagged the scones, Owen gave Alice and Franny a quick wink and stepped closer to the counter. "So sorry about Elmer," he said quietly. "I know you two were good friends."

Faith looked confused. "Elmer and—" She stopped abruptly. "Oh. Yes. Thank you. Very sad."

No one else was in the shop at the moment, so Alice lowered her voice and said, "We heard through the grapevine that Elmer actually wasn't such a good friend to everyone."

Faith gave her a blank look in response.

"Blackmail," Owen whispered.

Faith's cheeks turned pink. "Really? How terrible."

"So . . . He never bothered you, did he?" asked Owen.

"No," Faith answered. She paused and then said, "Are you three investigating Elmer's murder? I mean, if you are, that's great. I hope you find the person who killed him. But I don't have anything to contribute."

"We really are just here for the scones," said Alice, shaking the bag. "And we're not investigating, technically."

"We're just curious," said Franny.

"And I knew you were a friend of Elmer's," added Owen. "So, it occurred to me just now that you might know something more about him, or about whether he had any enemies around here."

"Sorry I can't be more help," said Faith, her smile returning as another customer came into the shop.

They turned to go, but just before they went through the door, Owen turned back. "That was some maze last night, huh? I mean, apart from the murder."

"I wouldn't know," said Faith, shifting her attention to the customer. "I didn't go."

A few steps down Main Street, they ran into Beau Boswell, Faith's fiancé, heading toward Crumpets. He and Faith lived in the apartment on the second floor, and had even followed Alice's lead and created a rooftop garden of their own.

Beau caught sight of Theo in his stroller and bent down to say hello to him.

"You can always get him to smile," said Franny.

"Babies love me," said Beau. "Probably because I'm funny looking."

"You are not!" said Alice. "I think babies just have a sense about people. Theo knows you're a good guy."

"We just bought scones from Faith. Have you two been able to take some time to go to the festival?" asked Franny, waving a hand toward the festooned Main Street.

"We have," said Beau, nodding. "Faith has afternoon help in the shop these days. We've really been enjoying all the holiday activities. Good job planning the event again this year, Alice."

"Thanks," said Alice. "I think I'm proudest of The Holly and the Ivy Maze. It's so much fun!"

"Oh, I know!" said Beau, chuckling. "Faith and I went last night. We got so turned around!"

"Did you find all three ghosts?" Owen asked. "Because we never did find the Ghost of Christmas Yet to Come."

"Neither did we!" said Beau, laughing and slapping Owen on the back. "I think we were getting close, but then we heard you scream, Owen—although we didn't know it was you at the time. Anyway, Faith was spooked and wanted out of there. We found a shortcut and skedaddled."

"Don't blame you a bit," said Owen. "We got out of there as fast as we could, too."

"Terrible, what happened to Mr. Smallweed," said Beau. "Hard to believe there's been another murder in our little town." He brightened a little. "But the police will get to the bottom of it soon, I'm sure. Those guys are on the ball." He winked at Alice and Franny. "I'd better be going." He was off with a smile and a little salute.

"So, Beau and Faith *were* there last night," said Franny.

"Yep," said Alice. "Why would Faith lie about that? And if she lied about being in the maze, was she also lying about her dealings with Elmer?"

CHAPTER 12

Arnold Zwicke's New and Used Cars was just at the western edge of Blue Valley. Owen was glad for the chance to take his SUV for a spin, since they'd generally walked almost everywhere lately.

"It's been ages since I've been out this way," said Franny from the backseat where she sat with Theo, who was happily gurgling in his car seat, shaking his favorite giraffe rattle.

"I know," said Alice. "I rarely go west on Phlox Street since the lake's in the other direction."

"So, let's go over our brilliant plan," said Owen as he came to a stop in an open parking spot at Zwicke's. "We act like Alice is on the market for a used car, and look for opportunities to feel Arnold out about his relationship with Elmer and his whereabouts last night."

"Got it," said Alice.

"All set," said Franny, shifting Theo into his sling carrier.

"Wow," said Owen, as they got out of the car. "This place has grown a lot. Looks like Arnold got a carwash."

"And a gas station!" said a voice from behind them. "Barney Potts," the man said, extending his hand. "Welcome in and happy holidays!" He pointed toward another corner of the lot. "Mr. Zwicke just added a convenience store, too. You can come here for all your automotive needs. Service, gas—why our little store even sells the best hot dogs in town."

"It's like a mega car dealership compound," marveled Alice.

They all introduced themselves to Barney and told him that Alice was in the beginning phases of shopping for a used car.

"You can't beat our prices," said Barney. "Honest Arnold is the best in the state."

He asked Alice a few questions about her price range and feature preferences, then walked them around the lot, showing them various models.

"This one's a real looker," he said, patting the hood of a sporty green car. "But don't let the cute exterior fool you. It can really handle the road."

"Does it get good mileage?" asked Owen.

"Oh, sure," said Barney.

"What kind of engine does it have?" Owen pressed on.

Alice and Franny simultaneously turned their heads to look at Owen—who knew absolutely nothing about cars.

"I believe this has an inline, six cylinder," said Barney, looking at the car.

"Can we have a look under the hood?" asked Owen.

Barney hesitated. "I don't have the keys with me, so I can't pop the hood at the moment, but let's look around a little more and then we'll see what you think."

They walked on around the lot, with Barney showing them lots of possibilities.

"He seems reluctant to get into the nitty gritty," Owen whispered to Alice as they moved from one car to the next, while Franny chatted with Barney about his grandchildren and when they'd each gotten their first teeth in. "He's all about paint colors and interior features."

"Makes you wonder," whispered Alice, nodding. "Could Honest Arnold be hiding something under all these hoods? We need to find Arnold and talk to him."

"First let's mention Elmer Smallweed and see how Barney reacts," said Owen. "If Elmer has been blackmailing Arnold, that means he's been out here a lot, getting freebies and collecting money. I bet this is where Elmer got that shiny new Cadillac he'd been driving around town. Let's see if Barney knows anything."

"Oh, Barney, I meant to ask," said Alice. "How is Arnold doing—I mean, I know he was friends with Elmer Smallweed, who got killed last night at the festival."

The smile instantly left Barney's face. "I don't think Mr. Smallweed was a friend of Mr. Zwicke's," he said.

"No?" said Owen. "I thought Elmer came out here to the dealership fairly regularly. Didn't he buy his car here?"

Barney's face was beginning to turn red—just like Faith's had. "Why? Did he say something to you?"

"Elmer? No," said Alice, confused.

"Because these cars are top of the line. Honest Arnold is the best. You can take that to the bank!"

"What? Barney, I—"

"Excuse me," Barney interrupted Alice. "I just remembered I —I'll be back shortly."

With that, he beat a hasty retreat toward the large showroom where the sales office was located. They watched through the huge glass windows as Barney went inside and found Arnold and the two talked. They quickly looked the other way when Arnold peered out the window at them. A moment later, he was stalking toward them, a stern look on his face.

"Hello, Honest Arnold," Owen said.

"Dispense with the chit chat," Arnold said, holding up a hand. "What did Smallweed tell you? Whatever he said, it's not true."

"We, um—" Alice began.

Owen stepped forward quickly. "Elmer has been saying that things go on here," he blurted out. "Shady things. Things that are . . . not . . . honest."

"That no good—" Arnold muttered under his breath. "I'm here to tell you that you will not find a better deal on a car than you will here at Zwicke's New and Used Cars. And you can take that to the bank!"

"That's just what Barney told us," said Franny.

"Listen, folks, I'm a car salesman. Sure, I show them off in their best light, but everyone does that. I defy you to find a salesperson who does otherwise!"

"Arnold, we know that," said Franny in her most soothing voice. "We didn't believe those things Elmer was saying about you." She looked at Alice and Owen for support.

"That's right!" said Owen. "We never believed any of it. You're Honest Arnold. Everyone knows that."

"And Elmer Smallweed was, well . . ." Alice searched for the right words. "He had a habit of using things against good people."

"You're darn right he did," said Arnold. "He dug up dirt like some kind of vermin. He figured out that I—well, that I sometimes embellished things a little bit, okay? And he held it over my head for years. Swindled me out of too much money. Threatened to ruin my reputation. Took everything he could get from me. I hated the man."

"Were you there—last night at the maze? When he died?" asked Alice.

"Yes I was," said Arnold without hesitation. "I was there with my wife. And in case you're wondering, no, I did not kill Elmer Smallweed. But you know what?" He pointed at Alice. "I'm glad he's dead!"

CHAPTER 13

"Daylight's burning, and we don't have much time. On to the last people on the list," said Owen, as they drove back to town.

"The Kingsleys," said Franny from the backseat. "Although after you spilled all those vitamins at The Daily Dose this morning, I'm not sure Sonny will let us through the door."

"Chances are, Sonny's still at The Daily Dose. So, let's start at the Good Earth Emporium," said Alice. "We can talk to Peyton first."

"And after this, we need to put our heads together and figure out which of these people we've visited today could be a murderer," said Owen. "Ooh—we can talk about it over more healthy snacks!"

"I don't think these healthy snacks are having the effect we'd hoped they would," said Franny. "We ate them all in one night."

"That's only because we were stressed and watching a horrifying movie," said Owen.

"Let's summarize the day," said Alice. "So far, Faith has lied about being at the maze when the murder took place, and she must've been lying when she acted like Elmer wasn't blackmailing her."

"And Arnold came right out and said he was glad Elmer is dead," said Franny.

"Well," said Owen, parking the car alongside Town Park. "Let's drop Theo off for his afternoon bottle and playtime at Grandma Bea's and then we can see what the Kingsleys have to say."

Alice's Mom was standing on the front porch of the cottage Alice and Ben had grown up in—and it was no wonder she and Martin had stayed there since they'd bought the place shortly after they'd married all those years ago. It was a charming little house on the corner of Trout Lily and Trillium, directly across the street from Town Park. It had a big front porch and a big backyard with large trees where Martin had created the bird sanctuary he'd always dreamed of. Alice had so many happy childhood memories of crossing the street holding her big brother's hand to go and play in the park while Bea cooked dinner in the evenings. And now another generation of Maguires would get to do the same.

"There's my little Theo," said Bea, holding out her arms to take her grandson.

The front door opened and Martin came outside and took the diaper bag Franny handed him. "Come on, Theo," he said, giving the smiling Theo a kiss on his fuzzy head. "You too,

Owen. I got a new birdbath out back with a moving-water feature. The rose-breasted grosbeaks are going to love it!"

"Wish I could, Martin," said Owen regretfully. "But we have some business to attend to first."

Owen and Martin were bird-watching buddies. They often went out into the field with their matching cameras and binoculars and lurked around for hours, watching for this bird or that. Alice often joked that Owen was the favorite child in the Maguire family—even though he wasn't technically related. He could be found trying new recipes with Bea in her kitchen on any given weeknight. He and Martin not only bird-watched, but had a regular card-playing group of which they were the founding members. And Owen had even taken ball-room dance lessons with Granny Maguire, and the two could cut a very impressive rug.

After saying goodbye to Bea and Martin, Alice, Owen, and Franny walked a couple of blocks down Trillium Street and turned left when they reached Azalea. A little bell dinged as they pulled the door of the Good Earth Emporium open. They were all relieved to see Peyton, but not Sonny, working there. She was helping a customer at the moment, so they got a small basket instead of a cart, thinking it might help them to avoid buying too many snacks this time, and browsed the aisles, all the while waiting for the customer to pay and leave.

As soon as the shop was quiet and Peyton was back at the counter, they took their basket forward to pay.

"I guess Sonny's over at The Daily Dose?" said Alice as she unloaded the basket.

"Yes," said Peyton. "Until we hire more help, he's over there pretty much all the time. I hate it that Elmer's gone, but this expansion will actually be great for our business. And Sonny says he's positive that Elmer would want someone to carry on with his mission to help Blue Valley stay healthy." Peyton paused. "I heard you were the ones who found Elmer at the maze. That must've been awful."

"It was," said Alice. "So shocking."

"Had you seen Elmer while you were in the maze, by any chance?" asked Owen. When Peyton gave him a questioning look, he added, "We're just wondering how it happened and who would've done such a thing."

Peyton seemed satisfied with this explanation. "No, I never even saw Elmer." She shivered. "I hadn't even thought about it that way. But you're probably right. Elmer might have even been killed while Sonny and I were in the maze! Do the police know when he died?"

"They're working on it," said Alice, wanting to keep things a little vague.

Peyton shook her head. "And we were having so much fun before we heard you scream, Owen. I got lost like I always do, but then Sonny helped me find my way again. He has such a memory for directional things. He never gets lost." She chuckled. "We're going to go again tomorrow afternoon in the daylight. I want to see if I can make it through without Sonny's help."

Just then, the shop door swung open and Darla Parker walked in. Alice knew Darla pretty well, since she was a regular customer at The Paper Owl.

"Hi Darla," Alice said.

"Oh, hello, Alice," said Darla. Then she turned a stern look toward Peyton and placed a half-eaten loaf of bread on the counter. "Peyton, I've narrowed it down. This bread is making me sick. It's not gluten-free, is it," Darla said this as more of a statement than a question.

"Mrs. Parker," said Peyton, pasting on a smile. "I'm sure if you're having trouble, it's because of some other ingredient—"

"It is not because of some other ingredient," said Darla. "I am gluten-intolerant. I have no other food allergies. I've gone through many loaves of this bread. You know I love it. But every time I eat it, I feel bad soon after. I thought it must be some other food, because I trusted you. But I have literally eliminated every other questionable thing from my diet. Today, I had a plain, dry piece of this and it made me feel *exactly* how I feel when I've ingested gluten. Now are you going to come clean about this or not?"

Peyton looked defensive for a split second, but then her face fell and she dissolved into tears. "I'm so sorry, Mrs. Parker!" she said. "You're right. There's gluten in the bread! Everyone raved about how good it was, and I felt awful for saying it was gluten-free. I've tried so hard to come up with a recipe that tasted exactly like this but without the gluten. I've been at it ever since I sold the first loaves and nothing works. I'm so ashamed!"

"Peyton, what if someone had gotten seriously ill?" said Darla, in a gentler tone.

Peyton swiped at her eyes. "I casually ask whether they have celiac disease before they buy a loaf. I say that there might be something in the bread that could cause a reaction so they don't buy any. Sonny says lots of people with other gluten issues can really tolerate a little bit, and that some people just *think* they have gluten issues but really don't." She looked at Darla. "I know that's not the case with you—"

"And it's not your place to take in upon yourself to decide that for people, Peyton," said Darla. "The bottom line is, you've been lying about what's in this bread, and that is wrong and could even be dangerous. When people find out about this, your reputation will be damaged, and we'll all wonder about what else you've been lying about."

"I'll make it up to you, Mrs. Parker," said Peyton, opening the cash register and refunding the bread. "And you have my word, I will not sell another loaf, ever."

"Peyton, the bread is delicious. You can still sell it. Just don't claim it's gluten-free."

"I won't, Mrs. Parker. Thank you."

Darla left the store, and Peyton looked at Alice, Owen, and Franny with stricken eyes, a tear rolling down her cheek. "I'm the worst."

"Peyton," said Alice quietly, looking to Owen and Franny, who nodded in agreement. "Did Elmer know about the bread? Was he blackmailing you and Sonny because of it?"

Peyton said nothing, but nodded rapidly, then grabbed a tissue and blew her nose. "How did you know?"

"We found out through one of his other victims," said Owen.

"You weren't the only ones," said Franny.

Peyton's eyes grew huge. "We weren't?"

Alice shook her head. "That Elmer was a real piece of work."

"He said that even if I stopped selling the bread, he'd tell everyone that I had lied about it and just like Mrs. Parker said, our reputation would be ruined. He even pressured us into helping to finance The Daily Dose. That's why we're desperate to keep it afloat. It's actually *our* money that's tied up in it. Elmer was supposed to pay us back, but we've never seen a dime. And Sonny was so afraid he'd ruin us, he wouldn't call Elmer out on any of it."

Peyton began to cry again, and they did what they could to offer comfort. By the time they left the shop, she seemed to be feeling better and had even managed to smile when Owen offered to work on bread recipes with her.

They walked next door to The Daily Dose and found Sonny, stocking the shelves.

"No offense, Owen, but could you steer clear of the vitamin jar?" he said, and everyone laughed.

"Just came by for some of that chocolate protein powder I saw in here earlier," said Alice. "The one with the superfood greens in it."

"Sure!" said Sonny brightly, going to the shelf and taking down a cannister. "Anything else I can get you?"

"No, that'll be all for today," said Alice, handing over her credit card.

"Be sure to come in for our New Year's sale in a couple of weeks," said Sonny. "We want to help everyone toward their healthy resolutions."

"Oh, we will," said Owen. "Hey—we'll see you over at The Holly and the Ivy Maze tomorrow afternoon. Peyton tells us you're going back for more."

Sonny laughed. "Yep," he said. "We were having so much fun there last night. I mean, until—"

Everyone nodded in understanding.

"I'm sticking to Peyton like glue this time," said Sonny. "She tends to get turned around. No sense of direction at all."

Alice, Owen, and Franny walked back across the park to the Maguires' and picked up Theo, then climbed into Owen's SUV.

"It's been a long day," said Alice. "Let's go home."

Owen eased the car into gear. "I'll build a fire and we can have a glass of wine and sift through what we learned today."

CHAPTER 14

The dulcet tones of the Gothic Trolls singing their rendition of *God Rest Ye Merry Gentlemen* were drifting up from Main Street as Alice warmed her hands by the crackling fire Owen had built in the fire ring on the rooftop.

"We have to tell Ben and Luke what we know," said Franny.

"I know," agreed Alice.

"Maybe there's a way to do it without giving Patrick away," said Owen.

"Honey, I'm home!" said Ben, coming out into the garden from his and Franny's apartment.

"Honey, I'm also home!" said Luke, a few steps behind him.

"Come warm up by the fire," said Alice, pouring two more glasses of wine.

Poppy, who had been lounging by the fire hopped up into Ben's lap, and everyone sipped their wine quietly for a few moments.

"Theo seems to be sleeping soundly," said Ben. "I took a peek at him when I walked through the apartment."

"He is." Franny nodded, patting the baby monitor that sat on the table. "Not a peep."

"Did he have fun with my parents today?"

"Oh, yes."

Ben looked at Luke.

"How was your day?" Luke asked, turning to Alice.

"Great," said Alice.

"Owen? Did you ever come up with a new plum pudding recipe?" asked Luke.

"I, um—yes, I did. I used butter instead of the suet and made some other adjustments."

There was a pause.

"Okay, what's going on here?" asked Ben. "What's wrong with you three?"

"Wrong?" asked Alice.

"Spill it," said Luke.

Alice, Owen, and Franny looked at each other.

"Okay, okay!" Alice finally said. "But first, have a scone."

She passed around the bag of Faith's eggnog cream scones and everyone took one.

"Wow, these are amazing," said Ben.

"Faith made them," said Alice.

"So, you stopped in at Crumpets today," said Luke.

"Yes—and that's where it all started," said Owen quickly.

"Where what all started?" asked Luke, setting down his scone.

"We bought the scones from Faith, and I knew that Faith had been friends with Elmer, because I'd seen her giving him free baked goods on more than one occasion," said Owen.

"So naturally, we said we were sorry for her loss," said Alice.

"And that was when she lied," said Franny.

"Faith? About what?" asked Ben.

"She said she hadn't been at the Christmas maze last night," said Franny. "But she had. Beau told us so."

"We know they were at the maze," said Luke. "Norman and Pearl Ann remembered them going in within our murder time window."

"But why would she lie about it?" asked Alice. "And why would she give Elmer free baked goods when they weren't really even friends?" Alice waved her scone in the air.

"And then we took Owen's car out to get gas at Arnold Zwicke's," said Franny casually.

"Why would you go out there? There are closer gas stations," said Ben.

"I was thinking of getting a used car . . . someday," said Alice. "But the point is, Arnold told us that Elmer was blackmailing him, too."

Luke sat up a little straighter. "He was in the maze during the window, too."

"With his wife, we know," said Owen.

"What did Elmer have on Arnold?" asked Ben.

"Let's just say he isn't necessarily always 'Honest Arnold.'" Owen made air quotes when he said this.

"And then there are the Kingsleys," said Franny. "We went to buy some more healthy snacks because we, uh, ate all the other ones."

"And Peyton admitted that Elmer had been blackmailing them, too," said Alice.

"Because her bread wasn't all that gluten-free after all," said Owen.

"Because her—are you serious?" asked Ben.

"So, what you're telling us is that you've been investigating Elmer's murder all day," said Luke.

There was yet another long pause.

"And we're supposed to believe that you just randomly stumbled on these suspects?" asked Ben.

"Okay, we didn't stumble on them. We found a list," said Alice. "We found a list at The Daily Dose."

"Elmer's list of people he was blackmailing," said Franny.

"And how did you find this list?" asked Luke.

"The point is that all of these people would've had motive to kill Elmer." Alice took a sip of her wine.

"And then there's Patrick," said Luke, looking steadily at Alice. "He owned the murder weapon. He was in the maze. What, I wonder, was his beef with Elmer?"

Alice felt her cheeks getting hot. "Patrick was the only other person on Elmer's list," she said quietly.

"So, Elmer was blackmailing Patrick, too," said Luke. "Why?"

"We—" Alice looked at Owen and Franny. "We'd rather not say."

"Why?"

"Isn't it enough for now to know that Patrick might've had motive to kill Elmer? Can you wait a little bit longer before you know exactly why?"

"A little bit longer?"

"Just one more day?"

"Let me be straight with you, Alice," said Luke, taking her hands into his. "We'd already discovered the kind of character Elmer Smallweed was. We didn't know he had that list —and your giving us that piece of information is very, very helpful. As to Patrick, neither of us believes he killed Elmer." Luke glanced at Ben.

"The only fingerprints on the knife were Patrick's, but the handle had clearly been wiped down. It isn't logical that Patrick would wipe off only the handle, since he knew his prints would be all over the knife—and even more, because he'd put that knife on display for the whole world to see. He'd never have used it to kill anyone. It'd be too obvious."

Ben shook his head. "No, the killer wanted us to *think* Patrick did it."

"Which is why we're almost sure he didn't," said Luke.

There was a collective sigh of relief from Alice, Owen, and Franny.

"Now. Can you show us this list of Elmer's please?" asked Luke.

Alice reached into her coat pocket, produced the notebook, and handed it over.

"Thank you," said Luke. "We'll talk later about how you found this." His voice was stern, but there was a hint of a smile in his eyes.

"Was the coroner able to pinpoint when Elmer died?" asked Alice. "I mean, had he been there long when we stumbled over him?"

"Not long at all," said Ben. "Zeb Clark's initial findings support what we already knew based on eyewitness reports. Elmer entered the maze at about seven o'clock. Owen screamed at about seven-thirty."

"Wow. That's a pretty short timeframe," said Alice.

"Which is a good thing, actually," said Luke. "It narrows the field significantly. The people on this list were all in that maze at that time—every one of them. Sure, it could've been someone else who killed Elmer, but these few rise to the surface."

CHAPTER 15

The next morning when Alice slipped into her wedding gown at Celebrations Boutique, she smiled at its perfect fit.

"You look like a magical fairy!" said Owen when Alice emerged from the dressing room.

"Or a princess," said Franny.

"Becky, it's perfect," said Alice, stepping onto the fitting platform and twirling around. "I can't wait for Luke to see it!"

"Exactly one week from today," said Owen.

"Be careful when you take it off, Alice," said Becky. "I'll get it all packed up and ready to go so it won't wrinkle before the big day."

Alice stepped off the platform and turned to go back into the dressing room, but then stopped. "Becky, have you heard anything lately about how Bella Hendricks is doing? Is she out of the hospital?"

"She's going to be just fine," said Becky. "Thank goodness!

She's home and still resting, but she's definitely on the mend."

"The whole thing was so strange," said Franny. "We were with her at the fun run when she fainted."

"It wasn't all *that* strange." Ethel Howard—Blue Valley High School's favorite English teacher and the wife of Doc Howard stepped out from a rack of dresses she'd been perusing.

Doc Howard had delivered half the population of Blue Valley, and Mrs. Howard had taught at least as many, so between them, they knew everyone.

"It was those gosh-darned diet pills she was on," said Mrs. Howard.

"Diet pills? Did Doc Howard tell you that?" asked Alice.

"He'd never divulge private patient information," said Mrs. Howard, shaking her head. "I got it from Bella's mother, who is hopping mad, let me tell you. She's telling everyone in town, in fact, in an effort to stop others from making the same mistake Bella made. Health food supplements, my patootie!"

"Wow, Mrs. Howard," said Owen. "I've never seen you this upset."

"After forty years of teaching high school students, it takes a lot to make me angry, Owen. But this most certainly does! That poor girl just wanted to look her best for her wedding day. But the whole world seems to be suffering under the illusion that only stick-thin equals beautiful, and Bella bought into that. If Doc Howard could've shut that Elmer Smallweed down, he would've," said Mrs. Howard. "And I know we shouldn't speak ill of the dead. But what a crooked, modern-day medicine man that Elmer was!"

"Mrs. Howard, did Bella's mother say exactly what it was she was taking?" asked Alice.

"Yes she did. It was the so-called *Healthy Weight* supplement from Elmer's Nutrique line. Elmer had made millions off that one product alone."

"Millions?" Alice sent a surprised look to Owen and Franny. "But Mrs. Howard, Elmer had *just* opened his shop a few weeks ago. How could he have already made millions?"

Mrs. Howard scoffed. "Because of his online business," she said. "He's been hocking that stuff for years. And he recently launched his *new and improved* formulations, which have apparently been problematic. You know, the FDA doesn't regulate things that are in the *supplement* category. Some nice packaging and a few phony customer testimonials, and you've got yourself a business. And people will pay anything for quick and easy solutions to their issues. And don't let those 'natural ingredients' claims fool you, either. Supplements can be mostly synthetic and still call themselves *natural* if even ten percent of the ingredients are plant-derived. And besides, 'nature' makes plenty of things that aren't good for the human body. Elmer's 'Healthy Weight' supplement was full of caffeine, and all kinds of herbs, including things like black cohosh, comfrey, ephedra, kava. Some of those can lead to severe hepatotoxicity."

"Hepa-what?" asked Owen.

"Liver damage," said Mrs. Howard.

"That poor girl!" said Becky.

"Bella was actually one of the fortunate ones," said Mrs. Howard. "In the past two weeks alone, a woman who lives in another region of Tennessee had to get an emergency transplant after acute liver failure because of those same pills. And a body builder who used the Nutrique *Bulk it Up* supplement is in the hospital. And worst of all, another Nutrique user—a young woman—didn't survive. She died three days ago. So, you see, Bella was actually lucky to have passed out at the fun run. She got the help she needed in time and now knows better."

"And they all got the pills from Elmer?" asked Alice.

"Yes they did," said Mrs. Howard. "Although Bella was the only one of those who bought them in person at his shop. The others were online customers. Mark my words, a slew of lawsuits are coming down the pike. Elmer would've been neck-deep in trouble if he were alive."

As Alice, Owen, and Franny walked home carrying Alice's gown in a long, zippered garment bag, they discussed Bella and her situation.

"Is there any chance one of the victims of Elmer's supplements killed him? Or maybe someone who loved them?" wondered Alice.

"You mean like Bella's fiancé or her parents? Or the family of the girl who died?" asked Owen.

"Let's ask Ben and Luke about this," said Franny, shifting Theo in his sling, and taking out her phone.

As she texted Ben, Owen's phone rang.

"Oh my gosh, this is the call we've been waiting for!" he said, looking at the caller ID.

"It's her?" said Alice, her heart feeling light again. "Oh my gosh! Answer it!"

Owen took the call, had a short conversation, and hung up.

"Ladies, we have a lunch date today," he said, smiling.

"With Sophie O'Toole-Sullivan?" asked Alice.

"Yep," said Owen. "The very one. Patrick's missing bride."

"Be sure to thank your cousin again for us, Franny, for tracking Sophie down," said Alice.

"Runesville is even smaller than Blue Valley," said Franny with a laugh. "It wasn't all that hard."

"We're meeting her at the park at noon for lunch," said Owen. "She sounded really happy that we called."

"Patrick's *wife*," said Alice, grinning. "I can't wait to meet her."

CHAPTER 16

"What did Mrs. Howard say Elmer's vitamin website is called?" asked Alice, sitting down at the café table in the garden with her laptop computer a few minutes later.

"Nutriquebalance.com," said Franny, sitting down next to her, being careful not to wake the napping Theo.

Alice typed the address into the search bar and a new window opened.

"Look at that website," said Owen, taking the seat on the other side of Alice. "So clean and polished. Anyone would think those products were legit. There are test tubes. And look—there's a man wearing glasses and a white coat. I can't believe these things aren't regulated."

"I know," said Alice, scrolling down the page. "I mean, some supplements on the market no doubt do exactly what they claim to do. But look at all these ingredients. They sound good, but we have no idea what they really do. And look at what all these satisfied users are saying." Alice pointed at one of the five-star reviews. "*I lost fifteen pounds in a month, and all I did was take Nutrique's Healthy Weight. I have tons of energy and feel better than ever. I am amazed at how easy it was!"*

"Yeah, you have tons of energy because you're all hopped up on caffeine," said Owen. "Go to the *About* section, Alice."

Alice clicked on the *About* menu at the top of the homepage and a new screen opened with a large photo of Elmer, looking a few years younger, standing in a beautiful forest, holding his arms out and smiling.

"It's all about Elmer and his background in the field of nutrition," said Franny. "Look—it says he studied holistic and plant-based nutrition at *top schools*. But it doesn't list the names of the schools anywhere."

"And it says he worked with doctors and scientists to develop his formulations, but it doesn't name any of them," said Alice.

"Our friend with the white coat and glasses on the homepage is probably just from some clipart collection," said Owen. He leaned forward a bit. "Hold on there, Alice. Scroll back to the middle of the page, where it talks about Elmer's credentials."

Alice did as Owen asked and they all read silently for a moment.

"There!" said Owen, pointing. "It says Elmer has worked for years with a silent partner who is also an expert in the field."

"Huh," said Alice. "So, Elmer had a partner." She read further, then reread the entire passage again. "It doesn't say anything more about his identity."

"Thus, the *silent* aspect," said Owen.

"I don't understand," said Franny. "What bearing does this have on the investigation?"

"Maybe none," said Alice. "But think about it. People have been getting sick from the new formulation of the Nutrique supplements. Someone even died. Like Mrs. Howard said, lawsuits are probably mounting. It's a scandal. Maybe Elmer was threatening to identify his partner to help ease his own burden of liability."

"Right," said Owen. "Maybe the partner didn't want his reputation sullied with the scandal, and killed Elmer before he could blab his name to the world. Or maybe the partner wanted out of the partnership, and Elmer wouldn't let him out."

Franny's phone vibrated, and she grabbed it on the first ring to avoid waking Theo. "Hi honey," she said.

A short discussion with Ben ensued, and when Franny hung up, she looked disappointed. "The police have already pursued the idea that someone who was harmed by Elmer's vitamins went after him. No dice. Everyone they were able to identify has an alibi. The most logical culprit, of course, would've probably been one of Bella's friends or family members, because they're local, and Elmer was murdered just after it came to light about what really happened to Bella. But they're all clear and accounted for."

"So that means it was probably one of Elmer's blackmailing victims after all," said Owen. "Or this silent partner." He waved a hand at the laptop.

"I told Ben about the partner too, as you heard," said Franny. "They're looking into it."

"We'd better get cleaned up and ready to go," said Alice, glancing at the time. "Time to head down to the festival and meet up with Sophie for lunch."

A short while later, they walked down Main Street in the direction of Town Park.

"What is that intriguing smell?" asked Franny, taking a whiff of the air. "I can't quite place it."

"Roasting chestnuts," said Owen. "I remember smelling them in New York as a kid."

"Look," said Alice. "It's coming from Kernel Pop's Popcorn Cart. I've never tried roasted chestnuts. Let's get some."

They got into the line at Ollie Watson's popcorn cart, and soon had warm paper bags of chestnuts, each one bursting from its brown shell.

"Tastes . . . not like what I expected," said Alice.

"This is like the plum pudding all over again," said Franny. "I thought they'd be, I don't know . . . nuttier. Crunchier. These are more like strange little potatoes."

"These take me back," said Owen, smiling and popping a chestnut into his mouth. "We'd buy a bag of these and a big soft pretzel from the stand near my parents' theater."

"Hi guys." Faith Lindor, who was walking hand-in-hand with Beau, emerged from the crowd of festival-goers. "I was hoping we'd see you."

"Hi Faith," said Alice, noticing the odd look on Faith's face. "Is everything okay?"

"Not exactly. But it will be," said Faith, looking at Beau for reassurance. "I need to tell you something. It's been weighing on me since I saw you yesterday." She cleared her throat and glanced at Beau again, who nodded encouragingly. "I, um, wasn't completely honest with you about my friendship with Elmer. I mean, it wasn't a friendship. The opposite, really."

"He was blackmailing you," Alice guessed.

Faith nodded sadly. "He dug around and found out the truth about my scones." She looked up at Owen with wide eyes. "I don't make them myself. I buy them and bake them off. I never necessarily meant for people to think I made them from scratch. But everyone just assumed! And then I gave in to temptation and took the credit. I feel like such an idiot! I'd been paying Elmer for a couple of years to keep my secret. He said he'd tell everyone that I couldn't bake a scone to save my life!"

"Oh Faith," said Owen, giving her a hug. "You run Crumpets almost entirely by yourself. Who could blame you for taking a shortcut or two? And those scones are delicious. Most people never think twice about who made them." He patted her on the back. "If you want to learn to make amazing scones, let's meet up in my kitchen. I'll help you make a scone fit for the queen herself."

"You will?" Faith's eyes filled with tears. "Thank you, Owen." She sniffled. "There's one other thing I was dishonest about," she said. "We *were* at the maze when Elmer was killed. We heard you scream, we heard people talking about what had happened, and we left in a hurry. All I could think about was that Elmer was gone—and at first, I felt a wave of relief. Isn't that awful? But then I thought that if anyone ever found out he was blackmailing me, maybe I would be a suspect. So, I ran away. I've been hoping that the killer would be caught and this whole thing would just blow over."

"It's understandable," said Franny, laying a comforting hand on Faith's arm. "Here. Have a chestnut."

Faith looked down at the chestnuts and took one. "Thanks, Franny. And thanks for understanding. I hope the police catch the killer. I hope that, wherever Elmer is, he's at peace."

CHAPTER 17

They found Sophie waiting exactly where they'd arranged to meet—at the gazebo in the park—and right on time. She was an attractive woman who looked to be in her early forties, like Patrick. She had pink, freckled skin, auburn hair, intelligent green eyes, and a lovely smile.

"I can't believe you found a Dickens-themed food truck," she said as they sat down at a picnic table with baskets of smoked haddock and crisp slices of toast topped with a cheesy Welsh rarebit sauce.

"Normally, that food truck is Picnic Patsy's Picnics On The Go," Alice explained. "Patsy can be found around the park serving sandwiches and potato salad most days."

"This is delicious," said Owen. "Who knew Picnic Patsy could be so versatile?"

"Hey, if Kernel Pop can roast chestnuts . . ." said Franny with a laugh.

There was a short pause as they dug into the food. Then Sophie took a sip of hot tea and tentatively asked, "So how is he?"

"Patrick? He's doing great," said Alice.

Sophie nodded thoughtfully. "Does he—I mean, is he . . . married?"

"Yep," said Owen. "To you."

At this, Sophie blushed and smiled. "So, you know our story."

"Are you . . . attached to anyone yourself?" asked Franny.

Sophie shook her head. "I know it sounds silly, but I made those vows to Patrick, and I've just never been able to bring myself to get out there and date. I mean, if I ever did find someone I wanted to marry, I'd have to divorce Patrick. And some part of me just doesn't want to do that."

"Haven't you been lonely through the years?" asked Owen. "Oh—sorry. Too personal a question."

"No, not at all," said Sophie. "I have a very full life. I'm a writer and a historian. I moved back to Runesville to be near my family because I work mostly from a computer in my home office, so I can really live anywhere. And I love being in the mountains. I get over to Memphis and some of the area universities from time to time to do guest lectures. Anyway, I stay busy, and I guess that's part of the reason I'm not lonely." She watched a little girl run past with her dad chasing after her and laughing. "Except sometimes," she said with a sigh. "Sometimes I think about the life I might have had."

"Did you ever think of getting in touch with Patrick?" asked Alice.

"I just couldn't," said Sophie. "I figured he'd call if he wanted to be part of my life. He never did . . . and I assume that's the way he wants it." She looked at Alice, a tiny glimmer of hope in her eyes. "I mean, unless he's told you otherwise?"

"I think it's time we took a little walk," said Owen, clearing the table and tossing their trash into a nearby bin. "We're going to show you a very special place."

They walked together down Main Street, Sophie stopping now and then to look around and say again how beautiful the town was. When they came to the Christmas Hound, there was a crowd gathered around, and Patrick's Irish accent could be heard above the buzz, saying, "No need to crowd, folks, we've got plenty for everyone. Careful, now."

Recognizing the voice, Sophie grabbed Alice's arm, and Alice patted Sophie's hand and smiled at her. On closer inspection, they saw that Patrick was serving his famous Christmas Irish Apple Cake with warm vanilla custard sauce.

"Oh. That explains the crowd," said Owen. "That cake is amazing."

"It's his mother's recipe," said Sophie quietly, nodding.

Owen raised his voice and called, "Hey, Patrick, how about a slice for Sophie Sullivan!"

Sophie turned beet red as the crowd quieted and turned toward them. Patrick stood there, frozen and wide-eyed, midway through drizzling sauce onto a slice of cake. The moment he caught sight of Sophie, his face lit up. So did

Sophie's. She released Alice's arm and made her way through the crowd, which was now watching in quiet fascination.

Patrick set down the custard. "Sophie."

"Hello, Patrick."

There was a moment of perfect stillness, then in one swift movement, Patrick stepped around the table, swept Sophie up into his arms, twirled her around, set her down, and kissed her.

"Wow," whispered Owen. "So, this is what it feels like to be Cupid."

"Well, to be fair, they were already in love," said Alice. "We just gave a little nudge where one was needed."

"Our work here is done," said Owen, linking arms with Alice and Franny. "Ain't love grand?"

They gave Sophie and Patrick a wave, and turned to walk back down Main Street.

"Just think, if Patrick and Sophie fall in love all over again, he can finally put his fears about being deported to rest," said Franny. "He really will be legitimately married to Sophie."

"And they'll both live happily ever after," said Alice.

"I see one of my excellent wedding cakes in their future," said Owen.

When they came to the Waxy Wick, they stopped to listen to the Gothic Trolls, who were out front, singing their cheerful rendition of *Ding Dong Merrily On High*. Marge and Koi gave them steaming cups of wassail and offered them cookies from a tray when they'd ended the tune. The Trolls thanked them and started off down the street to their next shop.

"You guys are doing a fantastic job," said Alice when they passed.

"Thanks, Alice," said Dante. "And thanks for hooking us up with this awesome gig."

"Yeah," Fenrir agreed. "We're having so much fun, and people keep giving us free food!"

"We want to be your carolers every year from now on," added Sía.

"You're on!" said Alice.

"Hey," said Owen suddenly, grabbing Sía's arm. "You three were at the maze the other night when Elmer was killed."

"That's right," said Dante. "Pretty scary, huh? I mean, like, we were all *right there*. We probably passed the killer at some point that night!"

"I know!" said Alice. "Gives me the chills just to think about it!"

"I remember you were caroling in the maze, and then you were up on that platform in the middle of the whole thing, right?" said Owen.

"That's right," said Fenrir. "We thought we could be heard better if we were right in the middle. That platform was the perfect stage."

"So, you could see all the people moving through the maze from there, right?" asked Owen.

"Pretty much," said Dante.

"Did you see Arnold Zwicke there?" asked Alice.

"Oh yeah," said Fenrir, snickering. "We saw him all right. He and his wife were off in a corner, smooching."

"Were they together the whole time as far as you could see?" asked Franny.

"Yep," said Dante. "They never left each other's side. Acted like two teenaged kids!"

"What about Faith Lindor? Did you see her?" asked Alice.

"Yeah, we saw them, too," said Sía, nodding. "Her and Beau, that is. They left in a hurry after you screamed, Owen. But they were already near the exit by then. We saw the whole thing."

"Did you ever see them separated, by any chance?" asked Owen.

"No. They were together. And like I said, they were clear across the maze from where you were with Elmer's body," said Sía.

"Did you see the Kingsleys? Peyton and Sonny?" asked Alice.

"Right again, Alice. We saw them, too," said Dante. "Remember, Fen?" he asked, turning to Fenrir. "That Peyton was so lost!"

"Yeah," said Fenrir, chuckling. "We were about to call out to her—tell her which way to go. But then Sonny found her and showed her the way."

"Was that before I screamed?" asked Owen. "Or after?"

The Gothic Trolls looked at each other thoughtfully.

"Maybe after?" said Dante.

"Or possibly before," said Fenrir.

Alice's phone rang. She glanced at the screen. "It's Norman McKenzie," she said. "I'd better take this."

They quickly thanked the Trolls, who tipped their top hats and walked on down the street, singing *Deck the Halls*.

Alice answered Norman's call and then hung up and turned to her friends. "Oh boy. He was calling from the maze."

"And?" asked Owen.

"And the three ghosts who were supposed to wander around in the maze today? They got spooked after Elmer's murder."

"Well, that's understandable," said Franny.

"Yesterday, Norman and Pearl Ann found substitutes. And Doug and Barb Blake and Marge Hartfield have volunteered to fill in tonight. But no one can do it this afternoon, and Norman asked if we could."

"Be the ghosts?" asked Franny. "Oh boy."

"Can Theo stay with your mom and dad for a few more hours?" asked Alice.

"I don't know about this," said Owen. "You know I get creeped out in that maze."

"But this time we'll be there in broad daylight," said Alice. "And it'd only be for a couple of hours, until Marge and the Blakes get there. Norman is really in a bind. He needs us to get over there pretty quick."

"Well . . ." said Owen.

"Please?" pleaded Alice. "If you do this, I'll owe you one."

Franny and Owen looked at each other.

"Okay," Owen finally said. "But I'm not being the Ghost of Christmas Yet to Come."

CHAPTER 18

As it turned out, Franny actually wanted to be the spooky Ghost of Christmas Yet to Come. As they drove to the clearing in Owen's SUV, she was already plotting how she would stand silently around corners and in shadows, ready to startle the next passersby.

"Franny, you're scaring me," said Owen. "And you just cackled a little."

"Sorry," said Franny. "But this is going to be so much fun."

They met up with Norman and Pearl Ann and quickly ducked behind the maze to pull their costumes on over their clothes. Owen, as the Ghost of Christmas Present, wore a sumptuous ermine-trimmed evergreen robe, a bushy mustache-beard combo, and a wreath of holly on his head. Franny wore a dark, hooded robe with a black face-covering that she could see and breathe through, but that completely obscured her face. And Alice, the Ghost of Christmas Past, wore a flowing white robe and wreath of flickering, battery-operated candles on her head.

"Do I look as ridiculous as I feel?" she whispered to Owen and Franny as they walked around to the front of the maze.

Owen sent a puzzled glance toward the wreath of candles, which was looking a little lopsided in Alice's red curls. "No, not at all."

"Owen James! I can tell you're lying."

"The maze opens in five minutes," said Franny. "I guess we'd better split up. We can't have people finding all three of us in the same place."

"Exactly right, Franny," said Norman, who joined them along with Pearl Ann. "Don't make it too easy for folks to find you."

"And when someone does find you, give them one of these," said Pearl Ann, handing each of them a basket filled with different sprigs of holly. "You all look perfect!"

"Well . . . I guess you're right. It's not as scary in here now, since it's not dark yet," said Owen as they stepped into the maze.

The wintery afternoon light was only just beginning to wane, but as the sun was already fairly low in the sky, the maze walls cast long shadows in certain sections, and it wouldn't be long until dusk settled in earnest.

"Let's pick sections that aren't that far apart," suggested Alice. "That way, we can call out to each other if we need anything."

"And we all have our phones, right?" asked Owen, taking out his cell phone and checking the signal.

"Yep," said Franny.

"I've got mine," said Alice, patting her pocket.

"Okay then," Owen gulped. "See you on the other side!"

With that, he walked in one direction, and Alice and Franny, after giving each other a little wave, walked down different pathways.

Alice could soon hear Norman and Pearl Ann laughing and talking with customers just outside the ivy-covered walls. The maze was opening up for business. Alice glanced at her phone. She, Owen, and Franny would only be covering the next two hours. Then Marge and the Blakes would arrive and take over. It wouldn't be so bad—and maybe Franny was right. Maybe it would even be fun to "haunt" the maze. Alice wandered down one green corridor, then another. She had no idea where she was, really, until she found the darkened corner where Elmer had died. At least, Alice was pretty sure this was that corner. She couldn't make out any remnants of blood on the grass, yet she felt a shiver run down her spine at the memory.

There were voices nearby, people laughing and remarking about how lost they felt. A little while later, the Gothic Trolls walked past, singing *We Wish You a Merry Christmas*. They waved at Alice and then disappeared around the bend. Then Samuel and Eve Berkley from the Valley Inn spotted Alice and collected their holly sprig before strolling off. She saw Violet Garcia from Violet's Blooms and Bouquets walking along with Lottie Ferguson, who owned The Green Thumb. After Harve and Sue Anderson from Cozy Bear Camp and Glamp stopped for their holly sprig, Alice began to loosen up. She was even enjoying reminding people to cherish their memories and spend time making new ones to hold onto for years to come.

She had just waved at Patrick and Sophie, who, to Alice's great delight, were walking through the maze hand-in-hand, when her phone buzzed. It was Luke.

"Who calls the Ghost of Christmas Past?" said Alice in her most ominous voice.

"Alice, are you in the maze?"

"Yes." Alice didn't like the serious sound of his voice. "What's wrong?"

"We found out who Elmer Smallweed's silent partner was. Sonny Kingsley."

"Sonny—are you sure? I knew the Kingsleys were involved with the vitamin shop that just opened. But are you talking about Elmer's online business?"

"Nutrique Balance, yes," said Luke.

"Wow. So that makes him a suspect."

"Yes—and he and Peyton were in the maze at the time of the murder. But they were together, and have vouched for one another."

"No," said Alice. "I mean, yes, they were together. But they must've been separated for at least part of the time, because Peyton got lost and Sonny came and found her. The Gothic Trolls told us."

"The Gothic Trolls?"

"Yes. They were up on the platform in the middle of the maze. They didn't see who killed Elmer, but they did see the various suspects. And they saw Sonny *finding* Peyton. Which means the two of them would've had to have been separated, at least for a little while." Alice thought for a moment. "And you know what? The Kingsleys were with us when Patrick showed us the key to the glass case that housed the knife. Elmer came up, waving that black notebook of his around." Alice sucked in a breath. "I bet Sonny saw that black notebook and knew what it meant! Maybe he snapped because Elmer had waved it around at him a few too many times. I remember Patrick setting down his keys when Taya came out and spilled the hot chocolate . . . Sonny could've grabbed that key in a flash." She paused. "Oh! You know what else? If Sonny is the silent partner, he would've wanted to stay out of the spotlight, because lots of lawsuits are probably coming down the pike. Mrs. Howard said so. People have been getting sick from taking Nutrique!"

"Nice hat, Alice."

"What?" Alice looked up and saw a shadowy figure leaning against the ivy covered wall.

"Hang up the phone." Sonny Kingsley stepped into the dim light of early evening, a sinister look on his face.

Alice fumbled with her phone and dropped it. When she started to bend down to pick it up, Sonny was there in an instant, grabbing for the phone. In the ensuing scuffle, Alice managed to kick the phone toward the wall, where it disappeared under a tangle of ivy.

"Who were you talking to just now?" asked Sonny.

"Oh, I was just . . ." Alice cleared her throat. "Where's Peyton?"

Sonny's eyes stayed glued to Alice's. "She's lost in here somewhere." He got close enough that Alice could feel his breath when he spoke. "But how lucky that I happened to find you at just the right time. Now. Who were you talking to?" He said this slowly, his voice low and angry.

Alice heard the Gothic Trolls singing *Jingle Bells* nearby— and from the sound of it, they'd brought their own bells—and for a split second, she wondered at how sinister a happy song could sound at a time such as this.

"It doesn't matter," she finally answered. "Because now we know what happened with Elmer, don't we?"

Sonny lunged at Alice, and wrapped strong fingers around her throat, almost completely cutting off her air supply. She panicked, gasping for air, clawing at Sonny's hands.

"He had it coming, Alice," said Sonny, his voice sounding too calm. "I did the world a favor, ridding it of Elmer Smallweed."

Alice frantically tried to nod in agreement, thinking she could try to calm Sonny down, but he was past being able to reason rationally. He was so full of rage. The light was dimming in Alice's eyes, and she had a vague feeling that it was ironic that she was going to spend the last moments of her life with a wreath of plastic candles on her head. But suddenly, there was a cry of agony and a lot of yelling mixed with a great deal of jingling, and Alice was released and fell to the ground. She sat up, rubbing her throat and blinking into the dim light to see the Gothic Trolls—all three of them—piled on top of Sonny. They were repeatedly hitting him over the head with their jingle bells, and by the time Owen and Franny came running, Sonny was begging for mercy.

Owen immediately called the police, then pulled Alice to her feet and enfolded her in a hug, which Franny quickly joined.

Once Alice had assured them she was okay, they all looked in wonder at the incapacitated Sonny, who was sprawled on the ground, the Trolls sitting atop him, and a crowd gathered around, ready to pounce if needed until the police arrived.

Then Peyton wandered around the corner. "What's happen— Sonny? Is that my husband on the ground? What's going on?"

Alice gently pulled Peyton aside just as Norman and Pearl Ann, who were now on the platform in the middle of the maze, guided the police—Ben, Luke, and Officer Dewey— into the maze to where the crowd had gathered. Soon, Sonny was arrested and escorted away, and Peyton, who had been shocked to learn of her husband's behavior, was taken in a separate car to make a statement at the station.

Alice breathed a sigh of relief when she finally stepped out of the maze.

"I told you mazes were scary," said Owen.

"Let's get out of these costumes and go home," said Franny.

Doc Howard came and checked Alice over and declared her bruised but fit as a fiddle, and after Alice had given a detailed statement to Officer Dewey, Luke caught up with her and told Dewey to get statements from the Gothic Trolls as well.

"Does it hurt?" Luke asked, gently touching Alice's neck, where ugly bruises were already forming.

"A little," Alice admitted. "These bruises aren't going to go with my wedding gown very well."

Luke smiled at her and shook his head, then kissed her and wrapped her in his arms. "My dearest Alice, you will be the most beautiful bride the world has ever known."

CHAPTER 19

"So, Peyton didn't know about Sonny's partnership with Elmer?" Alice was sitting in a chair in front of the mirror in the master bedroom at Luke's lakeside cabin while Franny did her hair.

"Nope," said Franny. "Poor woman. Sonny had been investing their money in Elmer's supplement business for years. She was under the impression that Elmer had been a friend of Sonny's parents, and that they were just helping him get his store up and running. She had no idea how far back that partnership stretched. She was mortified when Elmer called her out on the gluten in her bread—but that was just nickels and dimes to Elmer."

"And then the girl died after taking the supplements."

"Yes—there had been issues with the new formulations. Since Sonny was a silent partner, he'd had no say in the change of ingredients. Elmer guaranteed they'd see more sales. But then people started getting sick, and when the girl died, Sonny started trying to pull out of the partnership.

Elmer, of course, was furious, and manipulator that he was, managed to convince Sonny he'd be able to pin everything on him if he left the partnership."

"So, Sonny killed him."

Franny nodded sadly.

"What will Peyton do?" asked Alice.

"She's selling The Daily Dose property, divorcing Sonny, taking her half of the money, and keeping the Good Earth Emporium up and running. Turns out she's been the sole owner of the Emporium all along. She opened it before they were married." Franny coaxed a stray curl into place. "She's getting over the shock. She's going to be okay."

"We'll be her best customers," said Alice with a laugh. "We're all addicted to her cupcakes."

The door to the bedroom flew open and Owen hurried in. "The cake's all set up and it looks gorgeous if I do say so— Oh my gosh! Alice!" Owen rushed up and pulled Alice to her feet.

"Do I meet with your approval?" Alice asked with a smile.

"You're even more beautiful than my cake," said Owen, hugging her.

"High praise!" said Alice, laughing.

"Hey! Watch the hair!" said Franny. "Sit back down Alice. I'm not quite done. There's one curl in the back here . . ."

"Did Michael make it home?" Alice asked, looking at Owen in the mirror.

"He just got here," said Owen grinning. "He had a wonderful

visit with his family, and is home just in time for your wedding and Christmas."

"I'm so glad," said Alice, noting the happy gleam in Owen's eyes.

"Knock, knock!" Violet Garcia from Violet's Blooms and Bouquets stuck her head in the room.

"Come in," said Owen, hurrying over to help Violet with the large flat of flowers she was carrying.

"Looks like I'm right on time," said Violet, looking at Alice's hair. "All you need is this." She carefully handed Franny a lovely little circle of wintery greenery, which Franny placed over Alice's red curls.

"Smells like Christmas," said Alice, inhaling deeply. "It's beautiful, Violet."

Alice had chosen to wear the wreath of sprigged pine, spruce, and deep blue juniper berries instead of a veil, and seeing it now, she knew she'd made the right choice.

"All done," said Franny, stepping back. "You look perfect. Luke's going to be blown away."

Alice stood just as Ben entered the room. He stopped dead in his tracks. "This is not my baby sister," he said.

Alice turned and smiled at her brother. "It's me," she said, suddenly feeling the urge to cry.

Ben walked forward and took her hands. "Oh, Alice. Have I told you lately how proud I am of you?" Now Ben's eyes had filled with tears. "You were always underfoot. Always right behind me . . . And somewhere along the way, you went from being my pesky little sister to being my friend. So just in case I forget to tell you sometimes, I love you very much."

Alice and Ben smiled into each other's glassy eyes, but the moment was interrupted by a sudden sob. They turned to see Franny patting Owen, who had grabbed a handful of tissues and was blowing his nose loudly.

"That was the most touching thing anyone's ever said!" Owen wailed.

A group hug followed, and a few minutes later, with hair and makeup repaired, Alice took her bouquet and went into the living room, where her parents were waiting.

"Everyone's seated outside, and that sweet husband-to-be of yours has a roaring fire going in the outdoor fireplace. They're ready for you, honey," said Bea, beaming at her daughter. She squeezed Alice's hand and hurried outside to take her place with the small group of family that was waiting.

"Well, my girl, are you ready to get married?" asked Martin.

"Yes, Daddy, I believe I am," said Alice with a smile. She'd never felt more sure of anything in her life.

"By the way, I was told you still needed something borrowed on your wedding day. So, your mother and I are letting you borrow our song."

"What? Daddy!"

"It was the first song we danced to at our own wedding, and we thought it would be perfect for you at this moment."

Ben took Franny's arm and opened the door, letting in the sounds of the Gothic Trolls, versatile as ever and dressed in their wedding finery, playing *The Way You Look Tonight* on dulcimer, harp, and lute. Alice's breath was taken away as she stepped outside and looked around.

A fine, powdery snow had fallen during the night, but was beginning to melt as the morning sun crested the mountains and bathed the lake in golden light. Christmas trees covered in twinkling white lights were scatted all throughout the yard, adding to the magic. Ben and Franny made their way down the aisle between the few rows of chairs, and Owen followed close behind. All three were to be attendants to both bride and groom.

And there, at the end of the aisle, standing looking nervous next to Father Amos under an arch of evergreen boughs mingled with red roses and holly berries, was Luke. He looked up and saw Alice, and the nervousness melted away into a look of pure and utter joy. Alice locked eyes with him as the crowd turned in their seats. She walked on the arm of her father, trying with all her might to keep herself from breaking into a run toward the man she had come to love so dearly.

When Martin handed her off to Luke, Father Amos began the ceremony. "Dearly beloved: We have come together in the presence of God to witness and bless the joining together of this man and this woman in Holy Matrimony . . ."

The ceremony went by quickly in a happy blur, and more friends showed up as the reception got underway among the trees. Owen's cake was a vision of five pristine tiers as smooth and white as new-fallen snow, piled with cranberries that had been coated in sparkling sugar. Owen said the design was at once classic and dreamy—just like Alice. Alice and Luke cut the first piece and shared it.

"Owen, this is the best cake I've ever tasted!" said Alice.

Owen smiled proudly as Bea and Franny's mother, Pippa, hurried to the cake table to do the cutting and to distribute slices to everyone.

"Owen, it's perfect," said Michael, taking a bite. "I may have to write a poem about this cake."

"Do you hear that?" said Owen, putting arms around Franny and Alice. "My cake has now officially inspired poetry! It doesn't get any better than that."

A while later, Alice and Luke wandered down to the water's edge and stood looking out at the lake. Alice wrapped her cashmere stole around herself a little tighter. "Let's go stand by the fire," she said.

"Hold on, just a second," said Luke, stopping her. He took her hands into his and she instantly felt warmer. "I just want to tell you that you've made me the happiest man alive today." He chuckled. "People say things like that in movies. But it's true." He brushed a stray curl out of her face. "You have made me the happiest man alive." He said it slowly this time. "And all those promises we made today . . . I want to add one more." He paused and Alice felt like her heart could burst at any moment. "I'll never forget—I'll never take for granted—the gift of your love and your friendship." He laughed then. "I think I might've fallen in love with you the first time I met you."

"You mean when I ran into you and fell down onto the sidewalk?" said Alice, laughing as well.

"Yep," said Luke. "It sounds crazy, but since that moment, somehow, you've been it for me."

Alice stepped closer to him. "Who would've thought that bruised tailbone of mine would lead to this day?"

Their kiss was broken by the calls of Bea and Pippa, along with several others. "Alice! Throw your bouquet!"

"That's right," said Luke, turning to the table where Alice had set down her flowers. "You need to throw this thing."

Alice took the flowers and walked back up into the trees, where all of her dearest friends and family were gathered. "Single folks get over here!" she called.

She turned her back and flung the bouquet, heard a happy shriek, and turned to see the group of singles parting—and right in the middle of them was Owen, holding the bouquet.

"Well how about that?" said Alice, giggling.

"I can't believe it! I *never* catch the bouquet!" said Owen.

"Well, it's about time, then," said Alice, putting an arm around him.

Franny, carrying Theo, joined them. "Way to go, Owen!"

Alice put her other arm around Franny. "Two days until Christmas," Alice said, smiling. "After this wedding, we've all got a lot to do to get ready, you know."

"Oh, we're all coming right here to your house tomorrow night," said Owen. "I made gingerbread men and women, and Franny and I invited the whole family to come over for a decorating party."

"We figure we'll just keep right on celebrating," said Franny.

"And we've all been really good this year," added Owen. "I'm sure Santa will bring lots of presents."

For all the years of her life, Alice would remember this day. She wouldn't remember the words she'd said, exactly, but she would remember the promises she'd made. She would remember the tears in Luke's eyes, and the warmth of her own running down her cheeks. She would remember the exquisite beauty of the music and the mountains and the lake in this little corner of the world that would always be her home. She would remember the joy in the faces of the people she loved.

Alice looked around and smiled, shaking her head. "Santa can skip over me this year," she said. "I already have everything."

AUTHOR'S NOTE

I'd love to hear your thoughts on my books, the storylines, and anything else that you'd like to comment on—reader feedback is very important to me. My contact information, along with some other helpful links, is listed on the next page. If you'd like to be on my list of "folks to contact" with updates, release and sales notifications, etc.… just shoot me an email and let me know. Thanks for reading!

Also…

… if you're looking for more great reads, Summer Prescott Books publishes several popular series by outstanding Cozy Mystery authors.

CONTACT SUMMER PRESCOTT
BOOKS PUBLISHING

Twitter: @summerprescott1

Bookbub: https://www.bookbub.com/authors/summer-prescott

Blog and Book Catalog: http://summerprescottbooks.com

Email: summer.prescott.cozies@gmail.com

YouTube: https://www.youtube.com/channel/UCngKNUkDdWuQ5k7-Vkfrp6A

And...be sure to check out the Summer Prescott Cozy Mysteries fan page and Summer Prescott Books Publishing Page on Facebook – let's be friends!

To download a free book, and sign up for our fun and exciting newsletter, which will give you opportunities to win prizes and swag, enter contests, and be the first to know about New Releases, click here: http://summerprescottbooks.com